ISBN13 9-781943-437009
ISBN10 1-943-43700-9
Cover Art by Rebecca Poole

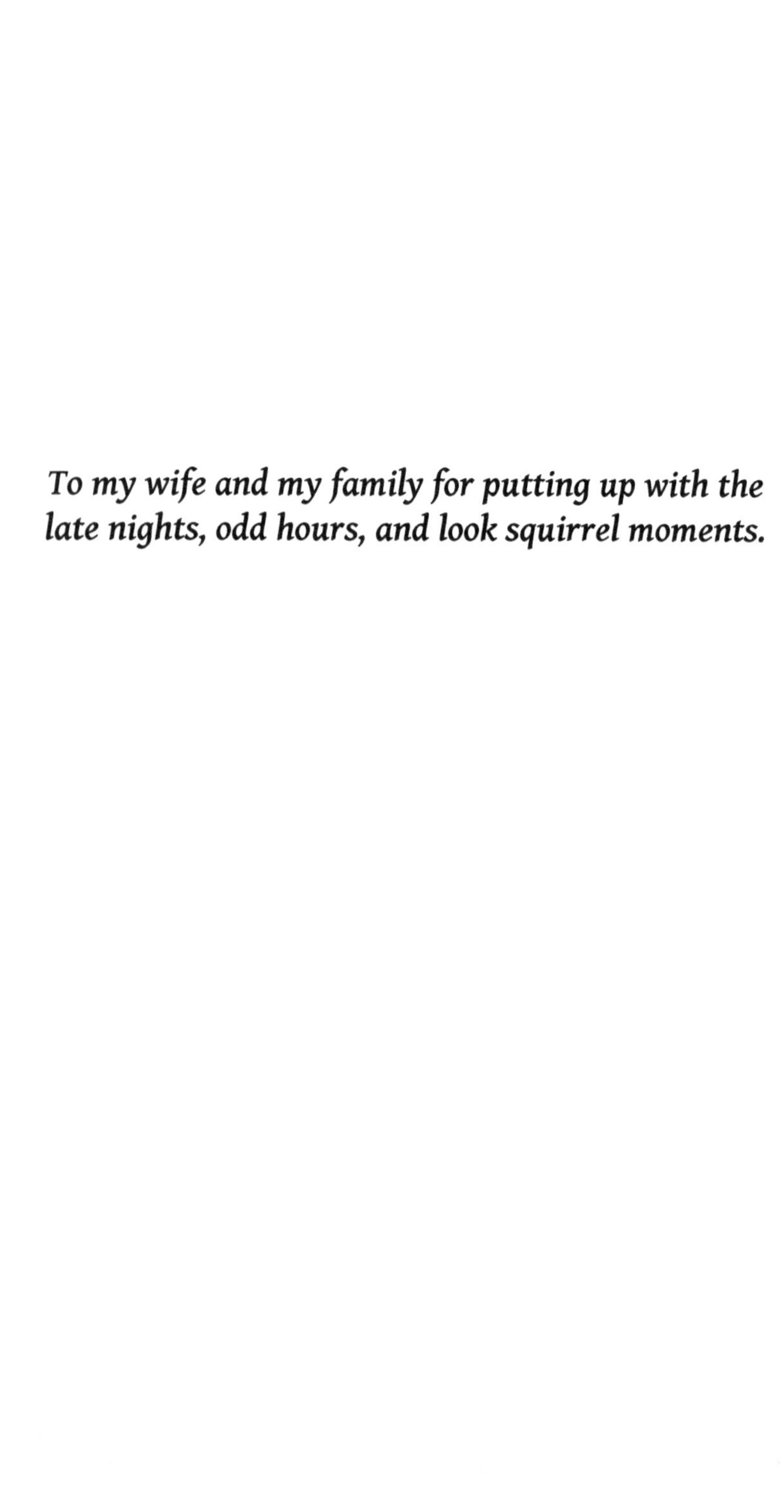

To my wife and my family for putting up with the late nights, odd hours, and look squirrel moments.

What's real can make the facts irrelevant

I was standing in front of the pile of dead bodies, the Scions were gone but the bodies were still just as dead except one. The little boy's face was looking around and his mouth was moving but nothing was coming out. I didn't want to see why. That's when the floating voice started. I couldn't pick a spot that it came from, just a floating sound that filled everything around me. "Your fault." over and over again in a little boys voice. "Your fault." I didn't kill them. It wasn't my fault that the Scions decided a mass killing was a good idea.

A second voice started. The new raspy voice was just a little louder. "Sacrificial alters, Sprite. Thank you for leading my little ones to such a marvelous playground."

THE LAST SPRITE
SPRITE SERIES BOOK ONE

CC Ryburn

Moral Imperative Publishing

CHAPTER ONE

Three-hundred and ninety days, Three-hundred and ninety-one nights. I don't need to watch over my shoulder, I just stay ready to fight at any moment. I tried running at first. I didn't know what they really were yet; I just knew that they're not human. I hurt one of them with what would have been a fatal blow to a person. He shrugged off the chair leg sticking through his chest and kept coming at me. Was it bad that I was the only one who seemed to see them for what they really were?

They called themselves "Scions". I looked it up once and it meant descendant of power or a plant that was spliced. Since they seemed more demonic than plant like, The type of fern wasn't applicable. The first time I saw them, they looked normal sitting in the restaurant. I barely noticed them they were so bland. They were just two couples, sitting with their food in front of them except none of them were talking, none of them were eating. They sat like a plastic doll family in their booth. Nothing creepy at all here folks.

For twenty-two years I lived a normal life, with a normal mom, a normal house, and more importantly normal friends. I even kept my hair the strawberry blonde that brought on years of grade school teasing. Twenty-one of those years, I spent in the same town. We never visited anywhere because mom was convinced everything we needed was right there. I had my volunteer work at the animal rescue, my friends who had also been born and raised there, and the handful of stores I visited regularly. When I was old enough to understand the concept of bills and responsibility, I knew why she didn't like leaving town. She was a single mom on a teacher's salary. I never saw Nashville except on TV until I graduated college. Mom just bought a house near mine. She had empty nest problems. If I took a job in France she would have suddenly had the urge to get a house there. Though she never left her house except for food and essentials. Mom's ideas of adventure stopped at the front door of her house.

I was eating dinner with co-workers, trying to unwind after a long day. The fact that today was my birthday came a close second to it being payday. I never really saw the sense in celebrating birthdays. They usually led to poor decisions and crappy gifts that never fit. The restaurant wasn't anything fancy, but it was convenient. It had the cheap booths of every chain restaurant, the dark carpet meant to hide spills, and the overly friendly wait staff. For the budget I had lately, that was a good thing. I knew my co-workers wouldn't let me pay, but I learned to never expect them to do it. Expectations had been a downfall for me through most of my life. If I planned it, it failed in the most spectacular way. The place did have the comfortable setting of a small town restaurant though. Maybe if I stuck around another year the entire staff would know me by name. Even with the warmth of the food and all the bodies packed in, I kept getting chills. I kept feeling like something was tapping me on the shoulder but there was only a wall behind me. I was getting creeped out enough to start thinking about going home alone. It was two blocks from here. I tried to blame it on the drink, except I hadn't touched it yet.

The server brought me my birthday dessert with some sparklers embedded in the middle throwing sparks and light in every direction. It pushed the ill feeling and dark thoughts away. I watched as all six co-workers sang their version of happy birthday.

George was still wearing his tie; each martini he drank seemed to magically loosen it a bit. Mike was already in playboy mode, flipping his sandy blonde hair casually, just in case no one noticed before how great his hair and features were. He alternated flirting with the waitresses and with Shelby. I didn't have the heart to tell him I had a better chance at dating Shelby than he did. His ego couldn't take it. Richard was our designated driver. He always volunteered to do that. I never worked up the courage to ask him why. Tony was laid back, but in a very confident way. I couldn't say I was completely immune to him. I must have done a passable act though, he never seemed to notice. Maybe that was what I liked about him. The new guy was hard to read. He didn't talk very much and had this way of looking through people. Psychopathic, maybe, but people that had his talent tended to move up the ranks fast. They sang so terribly it was funny. Before they finished their extended versions, a striking black-haired woman in the back of the row of servers moved just a little, making a gap in the group.

The light from my sparklers reflected off an old gas lamp hung on the wall for decoration. The light wasn't necessarily brighter coming out of the glass bell shape of the lamp but more focused. The two couples were illuminated for just a moment. When the light reached them, they no longer looked normal. They went from thirty year old's in all white-collar clothes, to something dark and wrong looking. Their muscles were too prominent, their faces no longer had pleasant smiles but were flattened with minimal skin showing and a black sinew mask topped with shocking white hair. They made my worst nightmares as a kid seem pretty by comparison. I glanced quickly around the room, a couple of well-dressed Hispanic men, a few black men with important looking suits, a few families here and there. Everything normal. I looked back where the light had focused and watched as the brunette with the mom jeans on, smiled in my direction. Instead of looking like a friendly smile though, it looked more like one of the animal programs showing fear and menace on the face of a predator.

I would like to say my escape was smooth with me slipping out of the bathroom unseen or some other slick move you see in the movies. I really wish I could, but the last things my co-workers saw of me was all ass and elbows with me screaming about monsters. I hit the door before anyone could react, knocking some poor older man down. I screamed apologies as I ran. My heart was racing; running had never been my strong suit. I knew the best thing to do when you felt threatened was to get out of that situation if you could. I just wasn't very good at it. I was always better at grappling. I kept my stride though; I had to make it to my house before those things could catch me. I'm not sure how I knew they were there to get me, or why I suddenly threw scientific thought out the window and believed they were real. I spotted my pretty yellow starter home three houses away and I poured on the speed. I got to my house not sure if I had imagined all of it or just ate one of Louis Carroll's magic mushrooms by mistake with my meal.

Mom jeans jumped through the sliding glass door and onto my shoulders before I even saw her. The glass seemed to be as much a deterrent as rice paper. Though I could see cuts covering both her fake and real body, her blood seemed to only fill in the now semitransparent body and the real body underneath re-knitting the black oozing sinew back together. There were flecks of glass in the tuft of white hair on the crown of her head. She held me to the floor with more strength than the MMA fighter that taught our last self-defense class. With her body mass, there was no logical reason for her to have this much leverage or strength against my shoulders. I couldn't get my shoulders off the floor while she held them. I was tall for a woman at six-foot one, but I wasn't all muscular, more comfortable than anything.

She let up on my right shoulder to reach back a hand that looked perfectly manicured on the outside and like a comic characters claws on the sinew inner body. I knew if she hit me with one of those I wouldn't have to worry about getting any crow's feet. I used what I knew of mass and balance and spun my hips out and kicked the bulk of my mass away from her. I'm glad my mom insisted I take so many martial arts classes. I just never thought I would need them for something belonging on a movie screen. You know, more of a bad guy in the bushes kind of thing. The Scion's hand slipped from my shoulder and I was loose. I rolled until I was out of her range and jumped up as fast as I could. She struck where I was before, and put her hand into the wood floor beneath. I ran two steps into the kitchen and started throwing knives from the knife block. Most of the knives hit her flat or with the handle, but somehow my big chef knife did what the other eight couldn't and sank deep in her shoulder. She flopped on the floor and I ran smiling, in spite of my fear, for being able to hurt her at all.

I grabbed my car keys and a broken wood leg that was left over from my co-workers rough-housing. I'm glad I didn't fix it yet. I almost got my phone out to call the police, but realized what it would sound like. "Hello nine one one, there are these demons from hell trying to kill me. Can you send someone to get them, maybe animal control or something?" I decided it was better to get some clothes and valuables and run like hell.

I heard two distinct crashes on opposite sides of the house before I could take a step. One was next to my bedroom, the other in the laundry room. I turned and saw the Scion that attacked me first, was still lying on the ground but clearly removing the knife bit by bit. The grimace, on her horrid features, made her look even more like a nightmare with her teeth sharpened to points and gleaming with spit. I sprinted as fast as my legs would carry me, jumping out of her reach, to get to the garage.

I ran down the hall looking back to make sure she wasn't following me. I was in luck, she was still struggling with the knife. I bounced off one of the males chests as he dropped from the attic

door next to the laundry room. My momentum
helped bury the wooden leg of the chair into his
chest deep enough that I know it was sticking out
of the back as well. I was planning to use it like
a baton, but I guess that works too. I scrambled
to get back up but instead of falling dead he kept
charging me like the drug-filled people you see
on the cop shows. Nothing told his brain that he
was dead and his body kept moving though slower
now with his left arm not doing much except
hanging there. He dove for me and I ducked back
down letting him go over my head. The wood
of the chair leg struck me in the scalp with its
jagged edge. I could feel the blood running from
the spot but not the pain. Adrenaline don't fail me
now. The Scion in the kitchen was getting back
to her feet, I could hear the sound of claws on the
hardwood floor. Then a gravely shriek behind me
that was barely speech at all screaming, "Get the
last. She is going to the carriage room."

I made it to the door in a full sprint with only
a light jacket, my purse, and car keys. Thank
God I wore flats today. I pressed the button to
unlock the car as I hit the garage, and pushed
the garage door opener button at the same time.
The dull light of the garage door opener gave
me just enough sight to pick out my car from
the things I never got around to unpacking. The
garage door was less than half up when several
things happened at the same time. I turned the

keys and pressed the start button, the door I just ran through was ripped from its frame, horrid screams of rage filled the space echoing in my head, and another dark figure crouched under the garage door as it was opening further. I threw my car in reverse and stomped the gas to the floor, it spun for a heartbeat on the smooth floor as three figures bounded toward the car like they didn't have to worry with things like gravity. The one behind me jerked her head up at the sound of my tires squealing on the cement. She tried to jump up to attack, but my wheels caught and the car spun out of the garage. She collided with the back of my car with a crunching thud and the sound of ripping sheet metal. That wasn't going to be covered on my insurance. My precious little red Mini wasn't going to look pretty with black ooze and claw marks in the lower trunk area.

CHAPTER TWO

My first instinct was to head to my mom's house. Even with our little family, Mom was always there for me. She may not believe any of it, but I knew she would be there for me. I was raised to only believe what I could prove. I could prove that I was hurt, but what I couldn't prove is beings, that didn't exist, had done them to me. As far as I knew we had no history of mental illness in our family. I didn't know much about my dad's side of the family. He died when I was really young and mom never mentioned any of his family members. I don't know why I never asked her once in twenty-two years about any relatives I might have roaming the earth. I didn't really know her side of the family all too well either though. I knew drunken Aunt Renee and poor Uncle Jeff who had the sense to run away and never come back when he realized what he got himself into by marrying her. Both of mom's parents passed long before I was old enough to remember. Now that I thought about it, they died within a year of dad. How had mom kept it together? I'm not sure I would have.

She kept a roof over our head even when the old house burnt to the ground. She had us in an apartment in less than six hours after losing our house to keep me in the same school. We lived in a few apartments and even a trailer for a while but she made sure I kept up my "self-protectin" as she called it. She never cared what martial art it was, she wanted me to learn some of it. Every time something bad would happen to a child she would point and say "See, I want you to kick their butt if they try that with you. I won't let anybody take my baby from me."

One of the large Scion's was actually trying to chase me down. I guessed he was the only one I didn't injure. I hit the gas and his image in the mirror started shrinking as I got my baby up to sixty. I made some ground until I slowed to turn toward mom's. I swerved and missed the Scion by inches. Somehow he knew where to cut me off. That meant he knew where I was going. If I went anywhere closer to my mom's house she would be in their line of fire. I jerked the steering wheel and took the first right heading away from her house. The Scion reappeared in my rear view, if I was going to get away from him, the interstate was the only place to keep this speed. I turned again and headed for I-65 south. If it took very long to get away from them, today being payday and my super car were my only blessings.

Every few miles I would change my mind and alternate between believing all of that stuff happened, and needing to get some medical help instead. Then I would think about the lengthy hospital stay involved and decide against turning around.

I stopped for gas at the northern border of Georgia. The station wasn't very well lit but the needle on my gas gauge didn't seem to care. Stretching my legs again felt like heaven. I could just make out the attendant in the store staring intently at the monitors on his desk. I was nearly halfway finished pumping the gas when my stomach decided to weigh in on the situation. I didn't get the uneasy feeling until I was halfway to the store. Part of my mind convinced me I was being paranoid and the earlier encounter was a horrible trick someone had played on me. All six coworkers singing their versions of happy birthday. No, actually only five sang. I'm not sure if the new guy even knew my name. I remembered his black hair, his general thin build, but I couldn't place his face now. That only increased my belief that something was wrong with my head. Was I having a nervous breakdown? I should be able to remember little things like that.

By the time I reached the shabby store, I was convinced it was all in my head. That didn't excuse my hunger though. I could just get some gas, chalk this up to a nervous breakdown of some kind and get back to work Monday. I picked up a pack of spicy beef jerky and some water and went to the register to pay for it.

The slimy feeling surrounded me. I nearly dropped my items on the counter as a full body shiver rolled from my spine to my head. The clerk didn't even flinch. He began automatically scanning my items never looking away from my face. That wasn't creepy at all. Neither was the leering smile. The smile didn't reach his eyes; it just hung there with his lips slightly parted. His lips were cracked and dry and his teeth looked like an ad for dental hygiene. His blue eyes and blonde hair were out of place with his darker complexion. My guess was colored contacts and a bad bleach job, maybe some strong drugs for good measure. He didn't say what the total was, instead pointing to the screen showing me the numbers. I looked down as I went for my wallet and noticed for the first time just how dirty his blue smock was. It had dark brown almost black stains everywhere. He was definitely not the clean type.

The moment I looked down to my purse to get my wallet something snapped my head backwards. I could feel something wrapped tightly in my hair and pulling hard. No one else had entered the store after me and it didn't make any sense until my gaze swept across the clerk again. The dark complexion gave way to a translucent ghost image surrounding a black sinew face, complete with shock white hair and violent looking blue eyes. I had no way to balance against the pull from behind me, so I reached out and grabbed for the counter. The smooth surface slipped through my fingers and my head and back struck the ground at the same time. I tucked my arm against my purse and tried to roll to the right but the hand holding my hair was wrapped tightly.

I got my body twisted just enough to see my attacker. If the ones that jumped me at my house were big, this guy was on steroids. In the bright lights of the store I saw something I missed before. The black sinew that covered him was actually moving not just re-knitting a wound, but moving around him in oil slick patches. What looked like corded black ropes before were more gelatinous and oozing. I fought the urge to be sick as I looked at something so horribly wrong. A fresh wave of pain helped. He pulled tighter and dragged me ten feet across the floor.

I could hear more commotion on either side of me but he had my hair pulled so tightly I couldn't look even if I wanted to. In my mind I was already working out their positions. I had to find a way out of this. The first thing would be to break his hold on my hair. If I didn't do that, anything else I did would be useless. The moment I stopped sliding I kicked both feet up and over, letting my momentum turn the movement into a double legged kick at his head. I missed his head and caught him in the throat instead. No matter what these things were, they needed to breathe. The sudden impact shocked him enough to let go of my hair and moved him a few feet back clutching for his throat.

I bounced when I struck the ground on my side,

I didn't think about sticking the landing after trying to be super gymnast. I got to my feet as quick as I could, being sure to stay out of steroid boy's reach.

I felt the attack coming before I actually saw it. It felt like black spots of tar arranged around me. Each spot was accompanied with the sound of claws on tiled floor. I ducked and rolled towards the only open area I could find. The one I felt coming first, crashed into one of the shelves. She managed to impale herself on the little hooks the candy hung from and stuck to them. She didn't even twitch as her body started just pooling into a puddle. I didn't even get a breath between seeing her hit before the one that was still wearing the ghostly image of the store clerk hit me in the middle of my side, driving me back to the ground again. I tried to tuck and roll with it but my head hit the tile hard. My vision blurred for a split second, it was still long enough for the other one to drive a fist into my ribs in the same spot. The shock of my rib breaking sent my adrenaline into overdrive. I had to get out of here. I didn't have any weapons, it was a three on one fight and I really couldn't imagine any way I might make it out alive.

I just started making a plan to deal with them individually, when another clawed hand came for my face. I wasn't even sure which one it was, I went on pure instinct and training. I managed to move my face away from the claws just in time and grabbed the arm they were attached to. I pushed as hard as I could on the elbow while pulling back with the Scion's forearm. A loud pop was the only satisfaction I got before I felt four claws rake down my back. My back was on fire with pain. I also felt something else burning. The hand I had on the Scions forearm had blue-white flames all around it and the flames ran across the Scion's body like I had poured gas on her. There was an unearthly scream and the burning Scion fell into the one that grabbed my hair earlier. Now he was on fire as well. The blue-white flames were scorching everything around, but I couldn't feel any heat from it. The one still wearing the smock stood still for a blink of the eye, Then he did something I didn't expect. He ran.

The store was quickly becoming engulfed with blue-white flames from the Scions. I wanted to find out more about who or what these things were, but if I didn't get out of the store fast, I was going to be trapped with them. I ran as fast as I could with the pain in my back from the cuts and a broken rib.

OK, run might be an overstatement, it was more of a hobble. I grabbed at the water and jerky as I went by the counter and headed for the door hoping the Scion in the smock wasn't waiting in ambush. Luckily enough, he wasn't. Had I actually scared one of them off? I was looking at my hand as I made my way to the car as fast as I could manage. It was no longer burning, and it really didn't look like anything had happened to it. My fingernails were all broken, but other than that my hand looked like it always did. I grabbed the door handle of my car and realized just how hard it was to climb into a car quickly with a broken rib.

I managed to get myself in and start the car. It wasn't very long before I felt the back of the seat growing wet from the cuts on my back. I sped off as quickly as I dared, considering I was leaving a burning convenience store and got back on the interstate. Now I had to figure out what those things were, why they wanted to kill me, and finally at what point I learned to become a superhero with flaming hands of justice.

CHAPTER THREE

I stared at my hand regularly during the drive, making sure I didn't go into fireball mode again and hurt my poor steering wheel. Every few minutes I would pick up the phone to call my mom and tell her all about my day. What would I say? "Hi mom, I know you don't even like fairy tales, but you should see what my hand can do." I imagined a million different ways to at least let her know something. I always called her. She was my best friend. I had no answers for any of the questions I knew she would ask. She didn't believe stories the news told her, I knew she would never believe any part of my story. I didn't have the words to explain how the Scions made me feel when they were close. I didn't know when or if I was coming home. Right now I didn't even know if I would make it through the next day. I would have to figure all of this out when she called me but for now I put the phone back down.

I managed to make it to Atlanta. The bigger city would let me get some help for my back and rib without drawing too much attention. I was following the blue hospital direction signs but at the last moment, I saw a huge church with lights all around it. I didn't really want to answer a million questions about how I had four razor blade cuts down my back, a broken rib, and fingernails that looked like I punched a wall wrong.

I have never been inside a church, but on TV

they always seemed to welcome the injured. I
didn't think to ask myself why a church was lit
up on the outside on a Friday night. When I got
closer I realized it wasn't just a church. It was a
shelter as well. There were signs directing me to
the soup kitchen entrance. I wasn't hungry after
all that beef jerky, but they were less likely to ask
questions. I know I wouldn't be the first one to
show up looking like crap and bleeding, maybe
the first one to drive up in such a sharp little car,
but they probably had medical tape and gauze.

I parked my car around the corner so it wouldn't
draw attention. I wish I had thought about the
walk before parking so far away. I could have been
an extra in a zombie show the way I was moving
and I was pretty sure the blood stain wasn't
coming out of the seat cover. When I got around
to the entrance there was a young looking priest
standing by the door. Two men with stringy hair
with backpacks went by and greeted the priest by
his name.

Father Michaels looked like a nice enough man,
though he looked young to be a priest. A little
on the skinny side, light brown hair, light brown
eyes, and a completely bland look to him.

Of course, all of my knowledge about churches
and priests were from mystery shows. Maybe they
were allowed to be younger and more rail thin
in real life. I nodded to the priest as I got close,
though I was still hobbling. He rushed over to

me, and for a moment I thought he was going to pick me up to carry me inside. I was spared from the macho chivalry when I put out my hand so he could just help me get my weight off my bad side. When we made it inside, I don't know what I expected. Huge gold crosses with shiny diamonds in them, a choir of young boys singing hymns, maybe a row of people with little cups of wine and wafers. I was beginning to doubt my perfect TV upbringing on the subject of religion.

The room was filled with old fashioned card tables, small folding chairs, and a smell strong enough to make me feel sick again. The combined body odor of the men, women, and even the children was bad enough. Seeing how dirty and malnourished some of them were just made it that much worse. For just a second I forgot about my rib and back until I put my weight down on that side again. The other thing that I noticed, every person was staring at me. Some with pity in their eyes, others with a more sinister look. All of them, except for one young boy. He glanced up and then right back down at his food. His dark hair hanging in clumps to cover his eyes. I felt like I was the star attraction at an old carnival. People continued to stare as the priest helped me to another room just past the soup kitchen. He sat me down on a hard plastic chair and drew a curtain at the doorway.

The room wasn't large but it was full of dressers

and an old red oak cabinet my mom would have killed for. It looked several hundred years old and every drawer and shelf looked well cared for. I noticed a plain wooden cross hanging from one wall but no other markings or pictures in the room. It was one of those crosses with the figure of Jesus hanging from it wearing a crown of thorns. It looked handmade but intricate. "What's your name child?" Father Michaels asked. I am sure he meant it in the best way possible. He wasn't going to win any points by addressing me as child though. "My name is Cheryl." I answered in a bit of a wheeze, "Do you have any medical supplies? I need to wrap this rib and get some gauze on the cuts." He looked at me with a shocked expression. I didn't say anything that warranted a look like that. Surely he had seen people beat up before. The streets of Atlanta weren't known for being friendly. "I will be right back Cheryl; we will get you fixed up and on your way as quick as we can." He turned and left the room in a hurry.

I was raised agnostic so I really had no clue if I had done something offensive. Religion was something my mom never talked about. I didn't know what to expect or what was expected of me in a church. I didn't cuss at him or anything. I was still working through it in my head, when another man who was much closer to the old tired looking priests I grew up watching on TV entered. He didn't really look directly at me but more around the contours of my body. I could see sparse hair on the dome of his otherwise bald head. His hands had a slight tremble in them, and were covered in age spots. One of his green eye's was almost milky white from a cataract. Then other seemed sharp and clear though. His gaze traced my outline. I vaguely wondered if glasses would help him focus.

When he spoke, his voice was strong and booming. He could have been addressing an entire audience instead of just me. "You are Cheryl?" he asked. He phrased it really odd. Though it was a question, it came across as a statement. "Yeah that is what my parents named me. Is that important?" "It is but only partially." I obviously didn't speak church. I had no idea what that even meant as an answer. He walked slowly over. "Let me see your wounds and I will get you healed up and back on the highway."

No one saw me drive up, I was careful about that. How did he know I was on the highway? How did he know I was still traveling? The word that really stuck was "healed" whenever I heard a priest use that word it was usually someone begging for money on the Sunday morning TV. "Whoa there, I just need some gauze for my back and some tape for my ribs. I don't have any money I can give you for your healing." I know it came across as crass, the only way I can explain it was the pain. I expected him to get angry, or defensive. I didn't expect him to laugh. It was a deep warm laugh of a much younger man. "No spr.. Cheryl, we would never ask you for money." There was something about the way he said "you" that sounded emphasized. The next thing I wondered was what he was going to call me instead of my name. He was old maybe he got confused. "I am sorry to have to ask this, but I need to cut your shirt off to see how bad it is. If it is a broken rib as you say, getting your shirt off any other way would be dreadfully painful.

My first reaction was to think of all the headlines about priests not acting so holy with the choir boys, but I didn't get that feeling from him. The rational side of me knew he was right. My mind was put at ease when he held up a sheet for me to cover myself with. The cuts on my back had gone through my bra, so the moment my shirt was off I could line up for a medieval painter.

His hands didn't shake once the entire time he cut away my shirt from the side with the safety scissors. He cut in a quick and precise manner. When he was looking at the cuts on my back he asked "How many of them were there?" He must have thought a gang of men had done this. "Four." I answered honestly. If you can't tell the truth, at least be honest. "This may be warm for a minute but it shouldn't burn." he said and rubbed something down my back across each cut. He had me look away as he did the same on my rib which seemed odd since it wasn't cut in any way. Then he reached up and ran it over my head where the chair leg cut me. I forgot about that one. I noticed when he brought his hand back down; there was no cotton ball or anything else in it. I thought about mentioning it, except whatever he had done had made my back much better, even my rib was feeling a little better.

He applied strips of tape to my ribs and then helped me put on a button down shirt from the cabinet. I didn't know how to react. Did he keep women's shirts in every size just hanging around? "I know you are in a hurry Cheryl. It was very good to finally meet you. In the matter of expedience, I have had Father Michaels put some supplies in your car for you. I got up and shook his hand, I wasn't sure if that was what I was supposed to do but it felt right. "Thank you for whatever you did, I feel better, though my rib will probably be sore for a long time." "No, thank you. I hope to see you remain healthy and succeed in everything." The weird factor jumped up a few notches with that. How had he known where my car was, how had Father Michaels been able to put supplies in my locked car, and "succeed in everything?" That would have sent the Scoobies scrambling.

When I came back through the soup kitchen everyone kept their heads down to their plates except the small boy who had barely noticed me on the way in. He watched every step I took with a bit of a smile. I couldn't get out of there fast enough. I noticed on each alternating step that the tenderness lightened and my stride loosened closer to a normal walk. I swore to myself that I wouldn't step foot in another church if they were all this spooky even if they could make broken ribs a minor inconvenience.

My cell phone would be good for another month if I didn't pay the bill. Then it would be turned off, I loved my phone, but I was in pure survival mode. I had no idea at the time how many Scions were out there. If I could get far enough away that they wouldn't be able to find me, maybe I could figure out how to make a new life. I didn't know how to change my identity like you see in the movies. The only thing I knew was to keep my eyes open at all times.

CHAPTER FOUR

Work clothes were great until you had to do anything physical. Finding my gym bag in the back of the car with more flexible clothing was the highlight of my day. Being able to get gas and some food without being blindsided was a close second. I managed to pick up a few more pairs of shorts and other gym clothes after making it to Orlando. It was Orlando, so shorts were better than the yoga pants I had in my gym bag. I had a few more sightings of the Scions, but managed to get out of town before they spotted me.

I swore not to stop at another church; I also recognized how short my money was getting. Eventually, my stomach overrode the creepy factor of church. I stopped to eat a sandwich at the first soup kitchen I found. I was getting used to the looks from the others. I wasn't dressed like most of the people there and I obviously took a shower recently. I had lost quite a bit of weight running with little to eat for so long. I didn't look malnourished, though my hair showed a distinct lack of nutrition. It looked dry and brittle to me, but compared to clumped and greasy, it still made me stand out as not really belonging.

I sat down to eat just as a priest came to sit beside me with his own sandwich. He was short, balding, and a sizable belly. His blue eyes looked haunted but still had that twinkle of hope. "Hello, we haven't seen you here before. What brings you to our fair world?" He said in a deep soothing voice. I thought about lying to him but instead decided brevity was a better option. "Just looking for a place to find some peace." I said forgetting my manners and speaking with a mouthful of sandwich. It was a good sandwich. He looked at me and smiled then turned back to his own sandwich and said "We get runners once in a while, if you need safe harbor, we can give it to you here for a little while." I realized he thought I was running from an abusive relationship, I guess that was kind of true, the Scions seemed to know me even if I only knew of them from internet searches.

I thought about turning down his offer. If, on the off chance that I wasn't crazy, these things from were from hell, I didn't have a safer place to camp for a day or two. "That would be great Father; just a night or two will be enough to let me get some kind of plan together."

I sat in the small room inside the church basement; one of the nuns came to give me some clothes donated by some wealthy member of the church. The names on the shirt tags were not something you saw on sale at the mall. I got a creepy feeling, not like when the Scions were near, just something not quite right. I slept well for the first time after the creepy feeling had passed. It was the first night I didn't have any kind of dreams, or at least ones I could remember anyway. I woke up and the sun was just rising. I never got up that early, but I didn't feel like going back to sleep.

CHAPTER FIVE

I walked around the church for a while. The stained glass on the windows was amazing. I had no idea who the people were, but I did get the feeling they were important. The one that really got my attention had Angels with trumpets flying through the sky and beams of light coming from each of them projected onto several small silver disks. The only full figure in the image was a man shining with a white light on a horse. I was so captivated by how much they managed to put into one piece of glass, I didn't notice Father Ryan appear beside me. "That is my favorite piece as well." he said without turning away from it.

"What is it?" I asked. Father Ryan blinked at me. "It's the second coming, Angel." I was confused for a moment, before I realized he was addressing me when he said Angel. To be fair, I never told him my name. "The second coming of what, some guy on a horse?" He blinked again, but this time added a smile to his expression. "The 'some guy' is Jesus Christ. Have you ever read the Bible Angel?" "No, my mom had me read plenty of books growing up but never a Bible." The surprise on his face seemed almost manic, except for the smile, it stayed the same. "In the Bible it says after the seven seals are broken and the righteous are taken to heaven, Christ will return to do final battle with the demons of hell and the Anti-Christ." I took all this in and wondered why anyone would want something like that. I liked the world how it was. I didn't want any more Scions running around, but overall my life had been pretty good. "Why?" I asked. Instead of answering me he asked, "Have you ever been saved?" I saw enough on the TV to know he didn't mean saving me from credit problems. "My dad had me baptized when I was a baby before he died. Does that count?" "Yes and no. Would you like to be saved before you leave?" I was getting that uncomfortable dark feeling again. "No I think I will be OK. Thank you though." He didn't argue or try to persuade me anymore.

He turned back to the stained glass. "Each seal is a torment; the first four are the Horsemen of the Apocalypse. War, Famine, Pestilence, and Death. Some people say those have already been broken." "You don't sound convinced." I replied. "No, I think they will be much more devastating than the things we see today. If we were anywhere close to the end of times, terrible things would have already been unleashed on this world." He stared at me unblinking when he said it. I did my best to not think of the Scions, I wasn't going to tell anyone about them. I would end up in some mental hospital for sure.

Something on my face must have betrayed my thoughts. Father Ryan smiled again and turned away. My comfort level was truly a memory now and it felt darker outside, even though there were no clouds. "I need to get some coffee." I said, changing the subject. "Is there any down in the kitchen?" I asked. "Of course there is, Angel. Would you like some company?" "No thanks, I can find it. I have coffee radar." I said and tapped my nose. I was hoping to lighten the atmosphere. The disappointed look on Father Ryan's face let me know I failed. "I will see you again I am sure, it isn't a big church." he said and turned to his right and started walking away. I went to the left to avoid any more awkward conversations.

I sat in my room with a big cup of coffee and a map. I wanted to make it to the Florida Keys for some reason, that was a thirteen hour drive at least, and I had just enough money for gas and tolls. I am sure the church would make sure I had food and water to drink, but I had already troubled Father Ryan far too much during my time here. I also didn't look forward to anymore dark feelings and awkward conversations. I thought about the Scions, my experiences in the two very different churches, and the possibility of just being nuts. I couldn't be sure I wasn't crazy, if I couldn't be sure, I knew no one else could either. I packed my small bag with the new clothes the nuns gave me and my toiletries. I looked back at the room and the completely bare walls. There wasn't a cross hanging in here, but I guess that was to keep anyone from feeling uncomfortable. I was almost ready to leave when there was a knock on my door. A very pretty young nun came in carrying a large bag full of food and water. I thought they would give me some food but this was enough for a month. I thanked the pretty little nun, she didn't say anything back but just smiled. I guess she didn't speak to heathens.

My Mini sat in the parking lot, clean and shiny again. Someone had washed it for me. When I got in to load my food and water I noticed they filled the gas tank too. I made sure to find Father Ryan, So I could thank him for everything. I felt better now than a few days ago. I owed him at least a thank you. He gave me a warm smile as he came in from his morning prayers. "Are you leaving us so soon? You can stay here longer." he said, though I noted it sounded almost rehearsed in nature. "Yeah, I don't want my pursuer to hurt anyone here. There are too many that can get hurt. I am sure you have better things to do than babysit an adult anyway." I said, giving him a way out of the generous offer. "Nonsense Angel, that is precisely what we do here. Take in souls that need something." He smiled again as we walked to my car. He gave me a wink and handed me a small paper wrapped package. He pushed me into the car before I could tell him he had done too much already. He just smiled as I drove off, with his brown paper package in the passenger seat. I didn't try to open it until I stopped for gas a few hours later. I had a feeling I knew what was inside,

I mean he was a priest after all. Sure enough it contained a plain old leather Bible with dog-eared pages and a thinness to the paper you only find on really old books. Inside the front cover I found several thousand dollars, a list of passages, and a word scrawled underneath. In hurried cursive "Sprite". I nearly turned around right then to return the money, it was far too much and I am sure others could use it more. I finally thought it through and decided I wouldn't win the argument anyway. Since the only part that made sense to me was Sprite, I went into the gas station and bought a soda.

CHAPTER SIX

I made it to the Keys probably faster than I should admit here. Florida frowns on things like admitting to traffic violations even in retrospectives. It really was peaceful in the keys, I went from island to island every few days. Taking time to read the passages listed in the front of the Bible. They all seemed to follow a theme. Angels and Demons fighting for the souls of men, epic battles between the forces. The night I reached Key West, I found some old fashion bungalows to stay in. I ate and read and just as I finished the last passage I fell asleep for the night with the old Bible still on my chest.

I woke up with my whole body prickling. I sat the Bible to the side and ate a sandwich and washed it down with some water. I packed my stuff still not feeling quite right in the head. I had the sense that something was watching me as I opened the car, then the inky black mass I felt at the gas station surrounded me. I wasn't sure how much more I could run now. I was almost to the end of my road. Before I could think about anything else, I felt the wind change direction and turned just in time to see one of the bigger white haired Scions dripping tar-like pools behind him in midair flying at my head, claws extended, mouth open dripping spit from a manic smile of shark like teeth. I tried to reach out and grab his chest as he came down to redirect him over me so

I could get away. It worked, well kind of, anyway. When I went to get in the car, I saw my hand was wrapped with blue-white flames, and as I looked past it to the Scion, I saw the blue-white flames engulfing him. That hadn't happened since the convenience store. I convinced myself I imagined it before. Two more came down on top of me burying me in their sinew and claws. I struggled and punched some more but so did they. The claws and the teeth tearing at my skin like razors. If they got many more hits in, I would bleed out even if I beat them. I caught ones wrist and pulled my head out of the way just before the other put her fist into the dirt where my head was. I locked the male Scions wrist and elbow and punched the other with my free hand, both burst into flames like the first. Screaming horribly right next to my poor Mini. I bet that isn't covered on insurance either.

I saw the last one on the roof of a cabana about to pounce but looking warily at the other three as they reduced to husks like those little black snakes we used to play with on the fourth of July. I heard her voice even though I couldn't see her mouth moving. "We have rid the world of all but one, do you think you can stand against us all little Sprite? We are but a few Scions'. There are thousands yet." I set my eyes on her and yelled. "Yeah, or you wouldn't be so scared to try me." She dove at a speed I associated with bullet trains.

She didn't think about the distance. Two hundred miles of hour is fast, but if someone has an hour to set up for it, you're going to get swatted down like a gnat. I spun to my left and grabbed her outstretched arm. I was intending to throw her as far as I could. Burning ash doesn't have much mass though. I watched warily as the flames turned her body into blowing ash in the wind. I spun and looked at the two by my car. There was nothing there either. My car looked perfectly fine. I looked around again, even the last one was gone now except a small ash mark. I got into my car and dug out the emergency kit and dressed my cuts with butterfly strips and bandages. At the rate I was going, I would look like a mummy if I had any more run-ins with them before I healed. I started putting stuff together as I drove to the end of the way south. I parked and sat on the hood drinking some water and watching the ocean waves. I guess I would need to rethink Father Ryan's message. I don't think he meant for me to drink a soda. That would be a stupid thing to put in an old Bible anyway. It wasn't like I was a spy with secret messages in soda cans. The Last Sprite. Guess that meant I had a new job now, wonder what it pays?

CHAPTER SEVEN

It didn't take long for me to realize how stupid it was to run to Florida. I was trapped with no way out down there. If I needed to escape quickly, it would have to be through whatever was attacking me. I prefer having options. I kept trying to think of the best place to go. The problem was, there was no answer. By the time I came to that conclusion, I was already in Huntsville. Everything I knew about these Scions was based on a few fights and some sketchy internet sites.

I stopped to grab something to eat besides sandwiches. The place looked one step up from a reality show diner. I just needed warm food, I didn't care if it was greasy and bad for me. I reached into my bag and pulled out the old Bible. I barely had it open before my server showed up. He was actually taller than I was, that was the end of his positive attributes. His hair was lank and greasy black. It wasn't even a natural black, his eyebrows gave it away. It got worse from there. His eyes were a crinkled set of slits. I wasn't even sure of his eye color or how he could see keeping them that closed. The fine lines on the side of his eyes hinted he was possibly way older than I thought, a heavy smoker, or both. The smell of stale cigarettes was choking in answer to my thought, even in the grease filled diner. The lines didn't stop with just his eyes, he had a frozen frown and lines to prove it didn't change often.

My stomach did a flip and I decided concentrating on the menu was better. "What do ya want?" Not much for conversation then. He glanced down at the Bible in front of me and I could see the disapproval on his face. I decided this wasn't my favorite town. Something about it gave me the creeps. I ordered my burger, fries, and some iced tea without looking back up. The air around me cleared of the stench and when I looked up he was gone.

I went back to reading the next part of the Bible on the list. Even if I was going crazy, the Bible could represent how to get my sanity back. That makes sense, right?

Either way, it seemed to be a logical resource for finding a solution. There was a distinct lack of Scions mentioned in the Bible. It talked about demon's leading people astray, but nothing about these horror film rejects. I also noted the absence of any demons in my travels. No one sprouting horns, carrying pitchforks, or showing the latest fashion in tail warmers. None of this made sense. The only logical conclusion was something bigger and badder than these Scions was behind it or, you know, the crazy thing.

Why me? I was a boring junior accountant. I wasn't going to fall down that well of thinking again though. The 'why me?' question consumed too much of my time already and never had an answer I liked. If I just took everything at face value, I found it easier to manage. Something horrible wanted me dead, I had the ability to stop it, I think. I just wish I knew who or what it was. The Bible was short on names of Demon's; it also didn't list very many Angels for that matter. The man returned with a plate and glass of tea. The unbreakable yellow plate had a crack in it and a stain on the bottom. I thought about sending it back to the kitchen, and then remembered all the horror stories of what kind of things were done to food that went back. I was going to say something but when I opened my mouth all I could do was ask for a straw. I took the greasy hot fries and dumped them into a napkin, then placed the napkin on the plate. I just finished wrapping the back side of the burger with another napkin when the server slung a straw on my table. He gave me a sideways look as he walked by; I guess he didn't like my appearance. He was probably sizing me up in case I skipped out on paying the bill. I tried to eat and focus on what I was reading, but the second bite of napkin wrapped burger broke me of the multitasking. I wiped my hands clean and put the old Bible back into my bag. I was either starved for real food, or this place made a decent burger. I had it gone and was taking another drink of the saccharin sweet tea when the server came back by and dropped a bill on my table without even glancing my direction. What a charmer I was today. I dropped a few bills for the food and tip and headed for the parking lot. I felt like I was being watched but it was getting dark and I couldn't see very far. I almost fumbled my keys as I unlocked the door. I knew better than to look like prey, but what else was I?

CHAPTER EIGHT

There was some kind of convention in town. Every hotel was booked solid. I was tired of sleeping in my car but it was better than driving while I was tired and full. I passed a rest area over near the diner and decided that was my best bet. There were cars parked in neat little rows with people sleeping in them. There is some comfort in a community, even if it is a temporary one. I got settled in with my seat reclined enough to sleep. I pulled out the old Bible and began reading where I left off in the diner. I only read a few lines before feeling like I was being watched again. I looked around and barely spotted a small boy looking out of a very old blue car. He was smiling at me. The pile of junk behind him gave me the impression he didn't have much to smile about very often. I waved, gave him a smile back, and then returned to my reading. If I ever get out of this mess, I really need to dedicate more time for poor homeless kids like that.

I woke to the sound of my car door opening and a waft of stale cigarettes and grease. I was still clutching the Bible as the server from the diner pulled at my legs dragging me out of the car. I started to scream, but before his face was level with mine, he had his hand over my mouth. I tried to bite his hand but I couldn't get my teeth into it. He already had most of his body weight leveraged against my arms pinning them to the dirt. "Do ya wanna pray first?" his breath was reeking of some cheap beer now as well as cigarettes. I couldn't answer with my mouth, but I let him know my intentions with a well-placed knee between his legs. I tried to fire up my hands but nothing happened. He wasn't a Scion. I had to do this the old fashioned way. He was scrappy for being so lean. The moments while I tried to flame up my hands he managed to redouble his grip on my arms and kicked one of my ankles hard. I let it sweep out and brought it back in for a kick to knock him off balance. If I could get his full weight off me I could roll out of this. The gravel of the parking area was digging into my back causing some pretty nasty cuts. Compared with the alternatives though, I was going to have to live with it. When my first kick failed, I twisted both hands to break them out of his grip. He would either have to uncover my mouth or give up holding my arms completely. His slitted eyes widened as my right arm came loose. That was all he had time to do. I struck with a side punch to his temple and another to his jaw before he let go of my other arm. He raised his hand to punch at me and I saw the shine of metal on his hand as he did. The brass knuckles would have fit in a noir detective movie, that didn't make them less effective though. I rolled and popped up as quickly as I could.

I have been fighting real things from hell so

much; I forgot how bad people could be. I dodged as he tried to charge at me with a fist swinging down. He might have a slight height advantage and probably strength as well. What he didn't have is experience and training. The clumsy overhand punch meant for my face gave me just the right angle to bar and pop his shoulder from the socket. The sound was terrible. He did what I wasn't able to before, he screamed. Out of the corner of my eye, I saw some heads barely popping over the edges of the car windows. Why weren't they getting out and helping me. Cowards.

The server made a guttural scream and drew my attention back to him. There was little left to see of him. Something had cut him in two pieces across the middle as cleanly as a razor. The top half of his mangled body was laying on the ground and the bottom half was at least three feet away both parts leaking blood in pools. I only had a second to look around before I felt them. There were four Scions here somewhere in the parking lot. It was so dark I couldn't see them but I could hear the crunching of metal and random gurgling sounds getting closer. I lost track of what dispensed justice so viscerally on server boy. Something sharp opened up my jeans and leg as neatly as a laser and then bowled me over in the gravel. The cut was like a trail of fire. I tried to jump back up, but my left leg wasn't listening. I balanced myself on my right leg, letting the left hang loosely to the side trying to listen for the crunch of gravel. In the pitch black, I heard the Scion as it jumped for another attack aimed at my backside again. I may have been weaponless against server boy, but these white haired Scions were becoming my specialty. I focused on the distance and direction of the sound. There were other random sounds but I needed to block them out to get this right. I timed it just wrong; the Scion was faster than I thought. I managed to twist away just in time to prevent major damage to my good leg but missed my grab for the Scions foot as it went by. I spun and hit the ground.

I was about to get up and changed in mid lift to collapse, carefully tucking my good leg under me. If these things wanted to fight me in the dark I could use that. Just as I expected the big Scion came closer to his lamed prey. Predators are intelligent and tricky, but they aren't wired right to be the prey. They don't recognize bait for a trap. The Scion was so sure his attacks worked he came close, too close. I waited until he stalked past me again with his side exposed. I used every bit of strength to push myself at him. What I didn't expect was the extra boost I got as I pushed off. I didn't know my own strength with all this adrenaline. I didn't just hit him in the side with both hands flaming. I bowled him over with more force than a car crash. I heard the muted sound of bones breaking beneath layers of cabled muscle

before he began bursting with blue-white flames.
I was so thrilled with my "win" I forgot about the
other three for a second. There was a high pitched
scream that broke my moment of triumph. If
they weren't attacking me in flanked groups then
what were they doing? They were hunting. Either
Scions had no sense of irony, or they reveled in it.
Hunting in Huntsville, I bet they would even live
somewhere like Devils Tower and fail to see the
folly of doing something so on the nose.

I found a fallen branch and lifted myself up
with the extra help. The branch was the perfect
height; I leaned on it and realized I had no idea
how to use a walking stick or a cane properly. I
was lucky growing up and never had the popular
cast signing party. The only time I came close was
when mean misses Johnston hit me with her car. I
managed to escape with some bruises and bumps;
she blamed me for denting her fender until
the day she died. Even at that age I tried to be
practical, if I had dented her fender when she hit
me I would've had more than bruises and bumps.

I did my best to figure the stick out. First
trying it on my bad side, that just made me
more unbalanced. I switched it to my right hand
and found I had much better balance this way.
I rushed towards the commotion. I didn't even
notice how badly my leg was bleeding. I reached
the area the sound came from and regretted
it. The bodies weren't all over the place like I

expected. They were in a pile. I turned away from the mass of faces looking out at me and vomited. I was about to turn back around to locate these monsters and make them pay for what they did, then I heard another scream from on top of the pile. They weren't killing them and then piling them up. They were carrying them to the other big Scion that was doing all the killing while standing on top of the pile.

I wish I could say I planned my next move, or even thought about it at all. I screamed until my throat was raw and pushed off as hard as I could. This time I didn't just fly a few extra feet from adrenaline, I launched like a rocket. The Scion dove down on the same trajectory. We were going to collide in midair. Just from a mass perspective that was a bad idea for me.

I wasn't dropping as quickly as he was. He might still be able to reach out and grab at me. If he did that, I could reach out and grab him as well. We got closer and I could see him reaching but he was falling too fast and I didn't need a refresher in physics to know there was some reason I wasn't falling. I was out of his reach as we closed, but that meant he was too. I did the only thing I could. I swung the branch down and used it like a club. I felt the change immediately. I wasn't flying at an angle anymore, I was flying straight up, and even more impressive was the speed he was traveling towards the gravel lot. He struck the ground and didn't break as much as liquefy on impact. I landed a few feet away from the puddle of ooze that had been the big Scion. Landed might give the wrong impression; it was a bit more of a spectacular crash. Lights popped in my eyes blinding my sight, and then everything went black.

CHAPTER NINE

Pain was the first thing that registered. My leg still felt like it was throbbing with each heartbeat. Confusion just added to it. I was in a hard bed with musty smelling sheets. There was an IV in my arm, but no hospital monitors beeping. The room had the feeling of a disused dungeon. Nothing on the walls made of stone block, a simple dresser opposite me and an old wooden door to my left with the tiniest bit of light showing underneath. The darkness hid anything that might help me learn where I was being held. I tried to reach out to feel for any Scions but it didn't work. I could only sense and feel things with my normal human abilities. I tried to get out of bed but found my leg in some kind of brace. That made things more awkward. I reached into the darkened corner at the head of the bed and grabbed the branch I used earlier. Before I got up, I wondered how I knew it was there. I passed out in a rest stop and didn't remember anything until now. Somehow I knew exactly where my walking stick was placed without looking. I used the walking stick on one side and pulled the IV tower with me in the other. My brain was still a bit scrambled. I fumbled with the stick and IV tower for a second, so I could open the door. I let go of the IV tower and grabbed the door handle. The heavy wooden door screamed in protest, but it opened. It knocked the IV tower over bursting the bag along with it.

Whatever it was set up to do for me was gone. I tore the IV needle and tape holding it in place from my arm. I am not a very hairy person, but the grip of the tape holding the IV needle in place made it feel like I was removing a layer of skin. I had to be ready, I had no idea who or what had brought me here. I didn't even know where here was. The door hinges squealing and the clattering of the IV tower's metal frame echoed off the stone walls of the hallway. I had to be ready for anything.

I hobbled my way to the end of the hall and peeked around both sides. They were both empty as well, doors scattered randomly down each hallway. I had to decide which way to go. "You shouldn't be out of bed Ms. Sprite." came a voice from behind me. I spun around and almost hit the priest with my walking stick. He didn't flinch. A young man, about thirty years old with reddish-brown hair looked back at me. He stood perfectly upright, even if that still only made him around five foot five. He had brown eyes and a baby face except for a scar on his left cheekbone that blended with his complexion well enough that it must have been really old.

"Who are you and how do you know my name?" I asked. He made a tsk sound but didn't answer me. After a painful second of silence he finally spoke. "I am Father Richardson; I pulled you from that parking area before I called the police on the two people killing everyone parked there. The police will find them don't worry." He never said how he knew my name. "The police won't be able to stop them." I said. He waited another full second before answering. It seemed to be his thing. "You took care of one of them. I saw you just before you hit the ground and passed out." I never thought about what my fights with the Scions would look like to other people. If I was the only one to see through their disguise, it could look really bad for me taken out of context.

Something else occurred to me, how he had rationalized me practically flying in the air after I sent the Scion to learn about impulse and gravel parking lots. If he thought anything was strange, he didn't show it. The implication that if a girl could stop them, the police could definitely handle them didn't get by me either. He had no idea who he was talking to. I could use that. I did a full body shiver at the thought of the bodies and realized I wasn't warming up. I glanced down and saw my leg was wrapped in sterile bandages and some sort of brace. I also saw there was a severe lack of pants down there. My favorite red panties were the only thing standing in the way of any modesty I had left. The priest didn't even look down once. "Where are my pants?" I asked as politely as possible. Well maybe not so politely. I took issue with anyone leaving me like this even in a private room, no matter what kind of collar they wore. Another second went by. "We had to cut them off of you to work on your leg." This was the second time a priest had played doctor and cut my clothes off to help fix me up. If this kept up my clothes budget would be higher than my gas budget. Gas budget. "What about my car?" Yet another second, "You wouldn't let us help you until we got your car out of there too. It is parked in our lot here."

Here, So I was some place close. I couldn't remember being conscious. I must have been though. He knew my name, he knew which car was mine, and I knew where the walking stick was even if I couldn't remember how. The pauses between answers were killing me. I'm sure Father Richardson is a good man, but talking like that with anyone for long would drive me insane. I started hobbling my way back to the room. The little priest didn't say anything but he stayed at my side the entire way back. I was really moving slow. I didn't have the fight or flight helping me ignore the pain and every step made my head spin a little. When we got to the door the priest pushed it the rest of the way open. The IV stand grinding against the stone floor as he did.

I didn't sit in the bed; it was more of a controlled fall. I put my weight on my bad leg just for a second and felt the world spin and all of the blood drain from my face. If I didn't get the pressure off my leg I was going to pass out. I was used to pain;

this wasn't even in the same zip code as pain. I had quite a few questions for the priest before I fell into bed. The dark tunnel of my eyesight was closing in though. I knew better than to fight it. The questions could wait.

CHAPTER TEN

I was standing in front of the pile of dead bodies, the Scions were gone but the bodies were still just as dead except one. The little boy's face was looking around and his mouth was moving but nothing was coming out. I didn't want to see why. That's when the floating voice started. I couldn't pick a spot that it came from, just a floating sound that filled everything around me. "Your fault." over and over again in a little boys' voice. "Your fault." I didn't kill them. It wasn't my fault that the Scions decided a mass killing was a good idea. A second voice started. The new raspy voice was just that much louder. "Sacrificial alters, Sprite. Thank you for leading my little ones to such a marvelous playground."

I looked around to find the source of this voice, I was willing to bet it was a demon, and even more willing to bet he had shockingly blonde hair. I couldn't locate him but I saw a huge stone the size of a car. Carved into the stone was one word. "Sacrifice." On the top of the stone I could see two feathers tied together. One was long and white, the other curled and black. The entire time I was looking, the homeless boys' voice continued like a drum beat. "Your Fault." Was it my fault? I knew I was being hunted and yet I chose a populated place to rest. Painting a target on everything around me.

Did this demon enjoy killing so much that

nothing else mattered? Was I putting everyone near me in danger? I screamed back at the voice, "It's not my fault." The smell of grease and beer filled my nose and sheer panic flooded my body with adrenaline. Hands grabbed each of my legs. I had to get away from here.

When I woke up I was covered in sweat, despite the cool air circulating down here. A few things had changed. There was more light now, and the IV was back in my arm. There was also a cup and a pitcher of water beside my bed. I looked under the sheet. Yup, still just the panties and leg brace covering my lower half. I could hear steps on the stone outside my room. I knew the whole thing was a dream, but my senses were still on overload. I grabbed the staff and prepared to use it like a club as soon as the door opened. Scion, Demon, or evil human, I was ready. I only had a split second of clarity before the door opened. The grease and beer smell were still in my nose. Reality was crashing in though. I pulled the staff back and rested it in my lap, you know, just in case. There was a light knocking at the door and no other sound. Just for a second I thought I imagined it. "Are you decent Ms. Sprite?" came Father Richardson's voice through the door. I wanted to say no out of spite, but something in the priests' voice put me at ease. He had a calm quality to his voice. It probably helped him sway the congregation during even the heaviest of sermons. He might have been short, but his presence filled the doorway. He was rail thin, I wondered if Catholic's fasted. I never thought to ask, but this was definitely the wrong time to go down that line of thought.

"When can I get out of here? It's cozy but," I looked around the stone block room in case he missed the sarcasm, "me staying here isn't good for any of us." With the light coming from the one window in the room I could see what I missed before. The priests lips moved in a jabbering motion for a second, then stopped. "Once your leg is healed enough to walk, I am sure you will find your way out of here easily enough. Can you tell me what happened the other night?" My first thought was his use of "the other night", how long had I been here already. My second thought was whether to tell him the truth and see how fast he had me committed, or make up something that fit better. He had a very upright posture and rigid face. I had I feeling the "demons are real and they want to kill me" line wouldn't work. I stuck with the facts, the attack by the grease ball from the diner, the four mass murders running amok through the parking area.

I didn't catch myself until it was too late. There wouldn't have been enough left of the first one to prove there were more than three. Crap. The look on his face told me he didn't miss it either. "I mean three, I'm sorry I am still dealing with everything and a little confused." It was only half a lie. I could tell he was working up to a question when his lips began moving soundlessly. I waited, I didn't want to. I wanted to yell at him to just speak up. Don't bother with filters around me, say what you mean. "What were you doing all alone and putting yourself in that situation?" I have heard about this line of questioning when a woman is attacked, I just never expected it from a priest. I wanted to say I didn't do anything wrong. Instead I found myself standing with the use of the staff and glowering down at the priest. Saliva was flying from my mouth; I couldn't have stopped it if I tried. "You want to know what I did. I kicked his ass. Is that what you want to hear? Then something bigger and badder than me split him like a hamburger bun." I wasn't sure what to expect from him. I think the look of shock on his face might have been one. Falling to his knees and crossing himself wasn't anywhere on my radar though.

It took me a moment before I noticed the lack of pressure on my leg. I was only a few inches off the ground. I was also surrounded by a pretty awesome light show. Bubbles of white and blue light surrounded me and my back hurt for some reason. I inhaled and blew it out slowly trying to calm my temper down. It seemed to work. I was back on the ground and everything else felt normal. I tried to get the priests attention, but his head was bowed in prayer or something. I reached down and put my hand under his chin raising it to look at me. "There was trouble, I took care of it. Let's just leave it at that." His pupils looked like a druggie's. I couldn't even see the color of his eyes.

"Thank you for your help, Now where's my car?" his lips began that muttering thing again. Instead of words though, he just pointed to his right. I looked around the room but there was nothing resembling pants. I did find my purse and my keys though. Somewhere, in the back of my head, I knew I wasn't being very nice to the people that saved me. There was another part that didn't care. I wasn't going be blamed if they got slaughtered during the next attack.

I hobbled my way out. The sound of the choir and the ten or eleven people praying in pews didn't escape my attention either. I just kept my head straight up and kept walking. Let them gossip. I am sure they would even if I was fully dressed. I got to the main doors and could already hear the mutters. Something inside me smiled. I wasn't sure I liked that part of me, but I couldn't exactly argue with myself. The wind had picked up, and it was still a little cold for this time of year. I didn't have much choice though as I slipped a pair of shorts over the brace on my leg. Goosebumps were threatening to turn into spikes on my skin if I got any colder. I made sure to turn the heater on high, took a second to regret not paying for the automatic transmission, and then headed west on the interstate, it was warmer that way. Less people too.

CHAPTER ELEVEN

I took a few tentative steps into the heat. I had the old walking stick, and the brace was gone leaving a really cute scar up my leg. I had no idea why I was in Yellowstone, I don't remember making a conscious decision to drive here, I just hit the road and kept going to what felt right. Last time I did that, I ended up in Key West. I was beginning to slip back into a mental argument due to a lack of Scions appearing. Funny, how the lack of something trying to kill you challenges your sanity. I noticed churches always running some kind of group function with food and clothes wherever I went. There always seemed to be a kindly priest at each that was expecting me. Thank goodness none of them were like the one in Huntsville. I couldn't complain about gas money, a shower, and a bed.

The driving was murder though. I had taken up doing Tai Chi again each night to stretch out my tired muscles. You wouldn't think driving and basically sitting all day would make you hurt so much.

I headed for the hot springs and when I was done there, I was going to see the geysers. I settled in, wearing the black and red one-piece I picked up in Florida. The water was rolling with heat over my tired muscles. I let it soak in until I was sure it would start cooking my insides. I climbed out and grabbed the walking stick and a towel I brought with me. I dried off my face, but as soon as I lowered the towel away from my eyes something in the distance moved. Coyote? Fox? No it was bigger than that, couldn't have been a Bear, way too fast. Then out of the corner of my eye I saw another one.

The walking stick started to smolder beneath my hand. I spun to look for the rear attack. What was that saying, Ask and ye shall receive, Yeah that was highly overrated. They liked getting your attention focused in one direction, while one of their companions closed the distance to attack. It was a good tactic for fighting four versus one. It always fell apart after I destroyed a few of them. They were kind of a one trick pony really. They would try to goad me into closing the distance for them or to get me riled up enough to make me burn up all my energy. It almost worked in Alabama, hence the limp. I was so tired after that fight I collapsed. I didn't recognize my body telling me when it was running out of juice. Now I knew what it felt like. I am pretty sure all of the seven worst curse words I knew could come out if I tried to describe it. If the priest hadn't decided to stop there, I would already be dead from the two remaining Scions.

Now I was looking at what was probably a strike team of four. Every time I had seen one of them, like cockroaches, there were more nearby. Each cell operated independently like bounty hunters that weren't into sharing things. They liked their group, but never banded together into larger groups. Good for me they sucked at team building. A bit of light flickered from the right. I instantly spun left; striking with my walking stick like it was a club. "Try that." I yelled as the flattened top of the staff struck the back of the Scions' horrid skull. I reached out on the same strike to rake her feet from under her. If I could get them off balance, they weren't hard to take down. Their shark teeth, black sinuous bodies, and extra-long limbs made them dangerous up close. The best defense I had was to keep my distance and try to catch them off balance.

No one had been able to tell me what these things really were. There were some funny conspiracy groups online, but only about half of the things they thought were true. If I was to believe everything the groups wrote about them, I would be under my covers with a flashlight singing boogeyman songs at them. The one I struck lay motionless, but I knew playing possum wasn't beyond them to gain the upper hand. They were really strong and could take a hit and keep coming. They had no sense of impending doom or any regard for their own well-being. I spun the walking stick to use the narrower end rather than the flat end, I drove it down toward the Scions' head but a mass hit me from behind. I flew at least thirty feet, scraping my arm, legs, and shoulder on the rocky clay. I felt my skin grinding into slick sheets of pain and I could hear the feet of the one that hit me turning around after passing me in the tackle.

I heard the one I had knocked down bearing in on me at a fast pace. I was near the top of a small hill and used it to my advantage. I shifted a little toward the slower of the two so I could time my strike; I pretended to be assessing my injuries instead of paying attention to the dual attack. I could smell a whiff of smoke from the handle of the walking stick and hoped they hadn't noticed. At the last second, I spun putting each hand out toward the attackers. Blue-white flame danced across my fingers, each one feeling warm. I caught one of the Scions by the arm, but the other one jumped at the last second and I swear she cleared me by twelve feet at least. I watched as she flew overhead in horrible slow motion. The other one collided with my hand and drove me a back a little before bursting into flames and burning into a charcoal like husk.

Being driven back is the only thing that saved my face. The drool coming from the one that flew over my head hit the ground next to me. It ate a hole through the rock and dirt. If it hit my face with the acid like spit, I would be blind and maybe dead. So, don't let them spit on you, check. When the one that wasn't screeching and burning hit the ground she bounced like a gymnast and did a back flip over my head. This was a new tactic too. Show-off, I felt like she was mocking my slower movement due to my leg. Before today, they had all stayed relatively on the ground. Of course, that was only counting for ten out of who knows how many. I was ready for the spit this time. The Scions seemed to be creatures of habit, if something worked, keep doing it no matter how predictable it was. If I believed the stories online, they were as old as the human race and the next best thing to immortal.

The next time she landed, I was ready and threw my hands out at her and watched the look of shock on her face as a gust of wind carried the fireball straight to her face. She burst into flames without me actually touching her. It took longer to consume her, but it also meant she wasn't within striking distance of me.

I kept trying to feel for the other two, but there was nothing there. I counted my good luck and grabbed my stuff and limped on my damaged leg. Now it hurt when I didn't put any pressure on it. I got back to my car, and oh God, my poor car. They had trashed it. The roof was peeled back with tatters of the Union Jack strewn about, the glass was all busted, one of the doors was ripped off and all the tires were flat. I was in the middle of Yellowstone, with a torn bathing suit, a towel, the walking stick, and the Bible Father Ryan gave me in the passenger seat. I started making my way to the main road to get some help. I listened and jumped at every sound. Then I heard the pop of tires rolling over small pebbles and stones.

CHAPTER TWELVE

There was something peculiar about my rescuer. He looked at me funny a few times. I guess a six foot one, twenty two year old woman with a bathing suit and a towel was enough to get that kind of peculiar stare. I pretended not to notice, as we wheeled our way to my hotel in his rusted pickup truck. He was tall and wearing clothes that may have been fashionable on the set of a western. People didn't actually dress like that on purpose did they? He had a lean angular face with jutting cheekbones. Ringlets of blonde hair were peeking out from under his baseball cap. I would be lying if I said the whole server boy thing wasn't popping into my head. He didn't give me the creeps, but right now everybody was suspect. The only reason I accepted the ride was the distance to the hotel. Ten miles walking on a bad leg would just make moving harder if I was attacked again. He hadn't said a single word the whole trip, that weirded me out some more.

When I got out he spoke for the first time since picking me up, "you forgot this." He reached to pick up the Bible, but at the last second just pointed to it. I grabbed it quickly not wanting to think what couldn't just hand me a Bible.

I went to the front desk and told them I lost my key. The eighteen year old kid gave me a new card without any problem and a smile I didn't want to think about. I was sure it was innocent; my brain just wasn't working that way lately. I got in my room and picked up the phone as I propped my leg up. Finally someone picked up the other end of the phone. "May I speak with Father Ryan please?" The lady on the other end of the phone seemed confused. "Who?" she asked. "Father Ryan, I was there a few weeks back and Father Ryan was running the soup kitchen and gave me a room for a few nights." I said getting a little testy. "Mam, we don't have a soup kitchen, we are a very small church. Father Chastain is our only priest for at least the last ten years." She said as though she hadn't heard the snark in my voice. I thanked her and hung up.

I tried to picture Father Ryan in my head, to make sure I hadn't imagined him. Maybe I really was losing it. I could see his short, slightly chubby, body, his blue eyes, and I suddenly didn't feel alone. I opened my eyes to see him sitting across from me. I flinched and almost fell off the bed. This made him break into a full belly laugh. I jumped up and slowly walked over to his still chuckling form. I reached out and touched his shoulder. He felt real. He laughed again. "I am as real as you are Angel." he replied to my nonverbal question. If he wasn't a human, what kind of Angel could he be, I thought they couldn't help mortals because of free will.

I told him about the run in I had with the Scions at the hot springs. He asked how many there had been. I told him I only fought two but they always seem to come in groups of four. He nodded. Then I told him about the strange man in the truck that wouldn't touch the Bible but quietly drove me home and made sure I didn't forget it. He just nodded, that was frustrating and not helping me to understand. I asked him why the man wouldn't touch it, was he some kind of demon? Father Ryan looked at me and said "oh he wasn't a demon, and I suggest you not cast him as such again. If he influenced you in any way he would change your path, thus he could only suggest you take the Bible. If he returned it to you unasked he would be pushing your path onto you. You aren't ready for such a thing yet. That was probably Gabriel, if I had to guess." he finished.

"OK so you're what? An ArchAngel?" I asked as polite as I could manage. He reached out and touched my sore on my leg and it stopped hurting. "No Angel, just think of me as lower down the path." he said. OK, mental note, look up Father Ryan online when I get a chance. He gave me a watery smile. His eyes crinkled but more in pain than a true smile. He tried to change the subject. "What are you planning next?" He asked. He seemed very interested in my answer, hanging on the silence like it was a cliff ledge. "I am going to consult the Bible again for clues, there must be something there if Gabriel, or whoever it was, thought giving it to me would change my future path. Then I am going to find the other two and take care of them." "Are you sure they aren't what are left of your Huntsville adventure?" I hadn't thought of that. That would mean they tracked me all this way though.

There were plenty of gas stations and deserted areas I rested in they could have made their move. "It seems like a long shot they would have waited this long. Unless, they didn't know where to look and just got lucky or tipped off somehow." I answered back. "How long is a day when you live an eternity?" I didn't have an answer to that. I didn't know if they still counted time the same. Just thinking about it made my head hurt. He truly smiled this time. "May I offer some advice?" he asked and without waiting for an answer he said "Keep the walking stick with you. You will find it useful plus they don't know that you are better already. It will make an excellent feint." Then he just disappeared. Not like in the movies with a poof or lights, he just wasn't there anymore.

I kept looking at all the passages listed after changing clothes into something a bit more comfortable. I read and read trying to figure it out. There were several passages about Egypt, Moses, and some about Noah but that wasn't helpful. I didn't know much about any of this stuff, I could be staring at the solution and not know it. I tried going through all of them again and then my stomach started complaining because I hadn't eaten anything all day. I went out to see what was nearby that I could walk to, my Mini was sitting in front of my door. Not a scratch on it. I looked several times over it and it was definitely mine. My stuff from Burger Palace was still in the passenger seat from the trip. The keys dangling from the ignition with my alien head key chain. I got in and drove to the nearest fast food, some small local chain of super fast burger places. I ate all the fries before I even got back to my hotel room. I was careful to use the walking stick in case I was being watched as I went back to the room.

I didn't know what I was supposed to get from the Bible, but I wasn't seeing it at all. Maybe it was a code of some kind that I didn't understand. They got my burger wrong, they put onions all over it when I told them I couldn't eat them. I took it back and got a replacement that I am sure someone made with loving care. They would never just scrape them off and microwave it.

On the way back I saw a dog dart in front of my car. I locked the brakes, going sixty miles per hour wasn't helpful even with my nimble car. I felt the hit. Crap, I hit some poor dog. I got out feeling bad for being preoccupied about a stupid burger. There was nothing there. Just my tire marks. Then I slammed into my car with so much force I chipped a tooth. It took a second for me to realize what had hit me and that the accident was a setup. I spun the walking stick like a baton. Being sure to look like I was favoring my good leg. It was darker out and hard to see them at a distance. I only had a split second to react. I dropped as one of them went right over my head. I was still worn out from the fight this morning and those two Scions were females. I could feel four oil slick patches moving in a circling motion. This felt like more a trap than an attack.

I tried unsuccessfully to burn them. I couldn't see them well enough to aim. One of them appeared really close to me flying through the air in a giant leap. I tried to duck as claws sank deep into my cheek. After passing me she extended her other hand and used her claws on my roof to slow her momentum down. "Bitch, stop messing up my car." I tried again to burn her but she was too fast. I heard the others coming too late and took another claw attack across the arm while dodging the other two. I was pissed now, she tore my new shirt, the first new piece of clothing I bought from a real store since this crud began. My car and my shirt were too much.

I leaned heavily on the walking stick and kept getting more and more angry. Before they could turn to attack again all four were being pelted with ice chunks while looking perplexed. I thought of all the other things I wanted vengeance for. I leaned harder on the walking stick. Four bolts of fire flew across the ground like blue and white snakes, two curved as the females tried to run and lightning blinded me for a minute. I could see the after image of them recoiling towards the ground. I walked to the strike areas not even hearing a whimper from any of them. I found the first one and I swear she was split neatly in half and on fire. I already knew what the other three were going to look like. The males must have been planning a second ambush when the females had me preoccupied. I looked up at my car. "That's right, don't touch my Mini." I felt the blood running from both wounds and my tooth was already hurting, at least it was a back tooth and didn't show. If this was a trap, or a test, I didn't want to stick around. I got in my car and went to the pharmacy and got some tooth medicine and more gauze.

CHAPTER THIRTEEN

All of the Scions seemed to attack in groups of four except once. I had no idea why that is, but it seemed a good round number. It felt like fighting one big foe that kept coming back after learning a way around my attacks and defensive moves. I stopped just outside of Phoenix. I felt like the further I was from a city center the better. After getting gas and some fast food I was back on the road. No problem. There is always a problem though.

I was traveling at sixty-five ish, I felt safer on the move. They couldn't keep up with me that way. I expected to meet more opposition coming out here. I didn't wish it would find me from the passenger seat of my car. A scion unlike anything I was used to appeared in the seat next to me and was already reaching for my hand before I registered she was there.

She had shiny black chit nous armor, spikes jutting out at weird angles and a cooler look in her eye's than the ones I was used to. She wasn't just calmer, she was more human like. I jerked the wheel nearly flipping us but it managed to throw her to the door frame. I could tell by the sound of the spikes slicing neat holes in my door. That pushed me over the edge. I grabbed a bare part of her arm with my flaming hand. It lit, but then flickered out. Her shiny body was charred where I touched her but it wasn't enough to reduce her to ashes like the sinewed ones. She cackled and swung the same arm at my head. I was trapped in my car driving, while something on the wrong side of a porcupine attacked me. I dodged the blow but not entirely. One of her spikes pierced my shoulder pinning me to my seat. She missed any bone but even the meaty flesh was sensitive. I couldn't move. I also knew driving and fighting wasn't possible. I locked the brakes and sent her forward. I had my seat belt to help me stay relatively stable but she didn't. She crushed part of my passenger dash with her head and her arm came free of my shoulder. The pain was excruciating but not being pinned to the seat made it a little better and a little worse. I tried to use my right arm to grab the staff. It wasn't listening to me. I snatched at it the second my hand left the seat belt release with my left arm. I bailed out just before she struck again with a spike that would have gone through my head.

I didn't have time to worry, I didn't have time to be indignant, she disappeared from the seat in my car and I felt something dark behind me. It was the same one. How I could tell them apart was anyone's guess. I knew it was the same one that just appeared in my car. I always thought of the Scion's as feral animals. She fought like a well trained soldier. Every time I struck at her, she disappeared. Now the entire staff was on fire but I still couldn't use my right arm. That wasn't helping my odds. I had to beat her quickly. I had less than a second to roll out of the way of another strike. I planned ahead and lead the end of my roll with a strong jab from my staff. She might have armor but it was still just armor. If I could get through it I could hurt her. She did exactly what I would have. She teleported to meet the end of my roll. The staff drove up into her past her armor. Little lines cracking with fire from the spot around the hole my staff made. She immolated on the spot. Well spots. She teleported away but each teleport was a little shorter than the last. Drawing it out like this had to be torture. She still kept doing it.

It wasn't until I felt three black spots near my back that I understood why she was willing to draw it out so much. She was the advance attack. Two males that had the spiky armor but another hundred pound on them both took swings at me. I rolled once again. The other female was waiting. She was just behind me. She might have more limits on her teleporting. It was still effective enough to give me a spike through the cheek. I turned my head just fast enough to avoid my entire head becoming shish-kabob. The fresh double piercing filled my mouth with blood. The metallic taste made me want to vomit; any sign of weakness was a death sentence.

I jabbed at her feebly but it was enough to make her teleport away. The two males lumbered up behind me and took another swing, this time down to cut me off from blocking in anyway. I tried to punch one but it was like hitting a wall. I spun to the side as the pavement buckled beneath their strikes. It gave me an idea but I didn't know if the staff could pull it off. I tried a lightning strike when I got my feet under me again. The two males moved out of the way of the snake like streaks heading their way. The female just reappeared next to me.

They were all attack, no defense. "What's the matter, a little red head has your spiky panties on backward?" I wasn't even sure if she understood me at first. Then a feral attack more in line with the sinewed Scions came from her as she dove at my face. I ducked and let her fly over my head in her rage. She struck both males. The spikes worked both ways, they were stuck. I smacked the staff down again and three snakes of blue-white flames flew toward them. A lighting strike came way too close to me. I ducked and covered and found only pieces of them when I got back up.

My shoulder and cheek were the only proof anything happened to me. My Mini had similar war wounds. It wasn't a matter of money; it was a matter of time. If I stopped to get them fixed I would be stranded in a public area. If I showed the neat little holes in my door and seats I would have a forensic unit playing CSI the board game on my car for bullet fragments. I knew none existed, but

I am sure they would find some anyway. I wasn't
always this jaded; I used to be a realist.

I patched the holes the best I could. I knew it
wasn't perfect by any means, maybe I could tell
them I went through New York once and they
wouldn't ask. I made it as far as a no name part
of Nevada. The weather was so warm I wanted to
plunge into a bath every time I stepped out of the
car for anything. I was tempted to find a place
to sleep during the day and drive at night. The
biggest flaw in that was the stopping. Anything
I did to stop was bad. I wasn't sure how I knew
it, but stopping could get me killed. I bought a
few extra bottles of water and threw them in the
passenger seat. It was tempted to bathe in them
right there. Get some of the red dirt staining my
skin off. I knew this also meant I would end up
with red mud, from the dirt on my skin, in my
socks and panties. Eww.

My shoulder hurt so badly but it was a clean
cut. Whatever the spikes were made of, they
were either super clean or my body fought
off the evil. Just a nasty hole, I could probably
drive through it, but a nasty hole anyway. I was
maybe ten miles down the road when exhaustion
washed over me. I tried taking another drink of
ice cold water to keep myself up. I was drifting
off. I never told my foot to stop accelerating, but
my car was sputtering and begging me to down
shift. I remember glancing down and seeing the

speedometer reading thirty miles per hour. I wasn't sure my car had even seen speeds this low outside of the occasional stop. The road got more blurry; I tried to get over so I didn't end up a splat on the news later. Then it just went black. I remembered the industrial sized water bottle slipping from my hands but I couldn't stop it. Sleep was better than the alternative. Hopefully it would take them a while to catch up. I saw something dark dart past but there was nothing else.

An eternity later the water bottle struck my lap and doused my shorts with ice cold water. The moment it touched my skin I jerked awake. Ice water to the crotch is better than any alarm clock. There is no off switch to the numbing cold. The water continued to pool in my seat under my butt when I noticed the shapes around me. There were four more spiky Scions standing around my car and I could feel a fifth bigger stain. It was oilier than the other four and much bigger feeling. I tried to push my door open and another of the big spiky ones pushed it shut so hard I wasn't sure it would ever open again. The two smaller ones kept making circles around my car, their human-like features, jabbering away as their spikes vibrated with each word. None of it was English but I knew what they were saying. "Sleep little one." Of course I get the evil nanny version of these things. I couldn't get out of the car.

At some point the engine had sputtered dead leaving me in a hotbox. They weren't going for direct confrontation. They were waiting until I cooked in my car. I grabbed at my staff but I had nowhere to strike the ground if I couldn't get out. These things didn't react as strongly to fire as the white haired ones. I was done for, I couldn't reach the ground, I couldn't burn their faces off and the two males were acting like body guards keeping my doors closed.

They weren't protecting the floor. They were only thinking in two dimensions. I was beginning to lull back to blackness, but I had to fight it back. I struck my staff down between my legs; if the spikes could punch a hole in my door maybe I could burn a hole in the floorboard. That also meant calling up fire while sitting in an oven. The rational part of my brain left as the water started to warm up beneath me. Either way I was going to cook. The greasy presence got closer, just as I struck down again I could see what looked like one of the white hair Scions in my rear-view mirror but he was taller, more emaciated, and much older. I'm not sure I can do five. Fine, target number three it was. I pushed every bit of rage, frustration, and anger into the last strike down. The staff punched through and the moment it touched the ground I could feel waves passing through my body, my brain was clearing, and three snakes of blue-white fire went flying out toward the two females and the old white hair. Only the white hair disappeared before the lightning came down and turned them into something that looked like a split lobster tail. With both females gone and the white hair nowhere to be seen the two males went mad. One tried to pick my car up while the other made a slashing motion with his arms at my passenger door. I took this chance to roll out of my car door and come up holding my staff in my good left hand. The nearest Scion swung for me and then dove. He should have kept himself upright. The moment he dove, he was at the mercy of gravity. His mass didn't matter, his ridiculous size didn't matter, and the only thing that mattered was redirecting it. I stepped to the side and drove the end of my staff through his back and skewered him to the ground. No lightning this time, just the sizzle of his insides cooking.

I was proud of finding a new way to kill them and before I could even finish making a smile, I was flying backwards. The other male raged and bellowed standing defensively over the husk of the one I skewered. I picked myself back up and struck out with my staff to take him off his feet. He wasn't any bigger than the one I already took down. He was just more pissed off.

He swung another hand at me. I managed to jump way to high for him to reach and turned the staff back his way. I blew him off his feet with a gust of wind. I flew backwards but managed a more graceful landing than he did. I had to get him while he was on the ground. If I gave him a chance to get up. No time for that though. I never saw one as big as him move like he was half his size and twice as fast. He was already charging me and I didn't have time to get away from him. I pointed the staff at the ground but at the last second I spun to the side instead of jumping up. I got super lucky; his dive would have hit me perfectly. If I just ducked his spikes would have turned me into a carved turkey. I knew better than to waste too much time thinking and kept moving. I had to get him off his feet again. It was the only time he was vulnerable. The second he hit the ground he rolled and popped into position like a seasoned martial artist. I wasn't fighting something big and lumbering, I was fighting a very oversized Bruce Lee, he came up toward me and I did the only thing left. I struck the ground again He wasn't more than ten feet from me when the lightning struck. The last thing I head was a guttural "Sun" coming from him as the horrid smell of burning meat filled my nose.

I went a month without any attacks after that, though I sensed them getting near several times. They seemed more disorganized, more feral and from what I saw passing a small group at seventy miles per hour, they were all the white hair Scions again. My shoulder was healing as I zig zagged around the southwest. I flew through the corner of Utah in one night; I had a bad feeling about heading any further north right now. I could use the cooler temperatures. I'm sure my poor car could too. I taped over the hole in the floor but I left it there just in case. Nothing would get me trapped in here again. Maybe I needed a proper break.

CHAPTER FOURTEEN

I limped from the car, using the walking stick. I still wasn't sure why I was here. I had no idea which side set this whole thing up. I should be better at knowing the good guys from the bad guys by now; of course the good guys rarely actually did anything obvious. I could hear the waves hitting the beach, no wonder people bought those sound effect machines to sleep to this. I looked at the bed and breakfast; it looked more like a Victorian house than a hotel. White wooden fence surrounding it, many of the large bright rooms were facing the ocean. I am pretty sure I could hit the ocean with a rock from here.

It was so beautiful, then like an electric jolt I reminded myself to check for the Scions. I stood in silence for a minute, the waves in the background, I could feel something. Whatever it was I felt was a long way from here. I relaxed a little, and returned to look at the house. It had been months since I started this trip against my will. I guess I impressed someone up there; I stopped having to scrounge for food and hotel money. Always some kind of happy accident left me finding the things I needed. I had a cell phone again, that was on the hood of my car in Bakersfield. I called the service for the phone and they had no record of who owned the phone but it was paid until next year. I couldn't help but wonder if that was a deadline for me or just a random date. I got a call on my phone as I hit Fresno to confirm my all-expense paid vacation here. I, of course, had entered no such contest but it was starting to feel normal.

I checked in to the room and what a room it was. I have never seen a place like this. The four poster bed was the size of a swimming pool compared to my normal beds. I put the walking stick in the corner of the room after closing the door. I haven't needed the walking stick in quite a while but, was told to pretend I still did to catch my enemies off guard. My life was so messed up, six months ago My biggest concern was that Jane was going to finish the coffee pot at work since she never refilled it. Now I had real enemies, They didn't just want to hurt me, they wanted me dead and gone. The worst part was trying to believe any of this was possible.

Maybe they are all aliens messing with me like a lab rat. I had an easier time convincing myself that aliens existed. These Scions with their shark teeth, razor claws, and white haired heads seemed alien enough. They were freakishly strong too. I don't mean they were guy who hits the gym twice a day strong, I mean comic character strong. What scared me more was who controlled them.

I wasn't a weakling anymore either though. When I first met them I tried conventional methods of destroying them. Knives, wooden spikes from a chair leg, even hitting them with a car. The part I was best at was running away. My new found ability to barbeque them was more effective but it really wore me out. It also seemed to have a limit. If I pushed past that limit, I would blackout then end up road kill if I wasn't lucky. I used my new phone to look up what a Sprite was. The internet wasn't much help. Sprite was an ancient name for an Angel on earth. I think if I were an Angel, I would know by now. I am sure there is scientific explanation to describe what I can do. My mom raised me alone and I never knew my father. She said he died just before I was three in totally normal circumstances. So it wasn't like he was the Angel. I haven't really read the Bible before now being raised indifferent to religion in general. Now I found the more I read certain passages, the more abilities I gained. Some of it might also have something to do with the funny markings on the staff. I looked them up as well, but since I wasn't sure what the funny curls and lines under each straight line were, it was difficult to find answers. It did have some cool tricks though. Hail, lightning, you know all the normal stuff. I was waiting to see if a bush would start burning and talk to me. I could honestly say, stranger things had happened to me. I walked to the bed and lay down. Listening to the waves crashing was putting me to sleep. I wasn't in any immediate danger and the bed was so soft. I didn't even get under the covers. I was out like a light in just a few minutes.

I woke with a start, not sure where I was for that brief moment. Everything came rushing back to me and I had a curious thought. I wonder what happened to my co-workers that threw me my birthday party. I thought about calling them to check in, then I realized how awkward that would be. They probably just thought I was in an asylum somewhere. The last they saw of me was running out of my own party screaming about monsters from hell. I didn't realize then how literal that had been. I opened the window and was met with a cool breeze and the smell of the sea as the sound of the waves was amplified through the room. A walk on the beach would be nice. In the middle of all this, I hadn't taken much time out for me. I just seemed to jump from one battle to the other. I hated the Scions, I hated that they took my life away as effectively as if they had killed me. My friends were gone, my mom was gone, and my job was gone. The only thing I had left was my Mini. At least I hadn't been dating anyone and left them behind to wonder.

Walking on the beach was cooler than I thought. I was glad I didn't just go "oh look a beach, I need a bikini." The steady wind was cool. I could see otters playing and could hear the sea lions on the wharf. There were funny birds that ran in and out with the tide like they were playing tag and of course seaweed, or I guess it was kelp, I don't know the difference.

I kept walking until I came to a man seated in front of a fire, for some reason, just for a second I imagined the fire being a bush talking to me. I walked by giving him plenty of space. I heard of people moving here just to live on the beach until they were moved on by the police. They didn't like the company of people, which led to fights when someone would get in their personal area. I got just past the man as he said "Good morning" to me. I wasn't sure if this was an invitation to talk, turn around and warm myself by his fire, or just a banal pleasantry. "Good Morning to you sir" I replied and kept walking. This seemed to meet his expectations and he turned back to his fire. I walked for another ten minutes when I reached a sign that said private beach. How can a beach be private? Did they have an accountant to make sure they weren't losing their investment by counting the grains of sand? I think they meant it too, I saw several signs up and down the beach staking their claim to the temporary sand.

I turned around, not wanting to get in trouble with the sand police. I was getting hungry, and needed to find food. Was it bad that I was craving seafood so near the ocean? Would that be like moving to a town and suddenly craving people's pets because they happened to be nearby?

As I was lost in this thought, I came back across the man with the fire. He joked "I thought I might see you again." he, no doubt knew about the signs even though they weren't visible from here. "Yeah, I didn't want to mess up any of their private sand." I replied with a small laugh. Did I just giggle, I mean he was cute, but giggle? I am not a giggle girl. More of a tomboy really. He beamed a smile at me of perfect teeth, shining like they were a light source. His eyes were dark like his hair but from this distance I couldn't tell what color they were. He had dimples; oh I loved dimples and a light caramel complexion. He was wearing a pressed white shirt with no collar and a wood bead necklace. His black pants looked equally comfortable but were also perfectly ironed with little creases down the front. Then he stood up, not bad. He was about six foot two, most men I dated were shorter than me, but of course I was six foot one. Any taller and I would have played women's pro basketball. "Hello, May I introduce myself, I am Juan Gonzales" he said with the words flowing off his tongue like one of the cheesy romance novels I read. Who says "May I introduce myself" anymore. One night in a bar I actually had a guy say "Hi, my name is Roger, wanna Fu..." I hit him before he could finish his sentence. He laughed and went back to his seat.

I could get used to Mr. gallant mystery here. I realized all this thinking put a hitch in the conversation and I was leaving him hanging. The hopeful look on his face was already turning to doubt. Crap. I didn't dare use my real name. I wasn't sure if that was dangerous or not, but why risk it. "Hello, I am Angel Billings." I immediately wanted to slap my own forehead and started turning red. Angel Billings, really? That sounds like a stripper's name, or a porn star. I was going to have to think of a better name for later and stick to it. Angel Billings jeeze. He still reached out for my hand and lightly brushed his lips on the back of it. My body went into overdrive. I realized I hadn't been touched so politely by anything resembling normal in over six months. Not that he was plain by any means, he was decent looking until he smiled, then he was handsome.

He invited me to sit with him though I don't remember the words actually being said. I was so nervous; I kept huddling up and running my hands near the fire to warm up. I listened to him talk about the environment and trains, and a multitude of things he was interested in. He tried to get me to talk about myself but I knew there was so much I couldn't tell him that it was hard to break the ice. We talked for an hour at least. He was such a charmer. He had a way of making you comfortable just listening to him.

My stomach gurgled; I used that as an excuse to break off for now and promised to come back after a while. He said he had some stuff to take care of as well and would see me in a few hours. He leaned in to kiss my cheek, I don't know what made me do it, I must be losing it, I just met him, but I turned my head at the last moment and met him with a kiss of my own, full of the lips. He was slightly shocked, but softened his kiss to match mine. He put his hands in my hair caressing my head as we kissed. Then something didn't feel right, like something slimy ran down my back and the kiss changed. More ferocious, more pressure. I ripped my head back and lost a few hairs in the sudden movement. I looked back at Juan, he was there, but underneath was the black shadow moving in strange watery motions.

CHAPTER FIFTEEN

I pulled back from Juan as fast as my legs would let me, he just sat there. He wasn't attacking or doing anything. I felt around for more of them. With few exceptions they had always been in groups of four. One all alone would be easy to take care of, or so I was thinking. Juan still smiled at me with the comfort he wore before I saw through his disguise. I could still see a little of his inner self but not nearly as much as I had when we were close. I was only ten feet away from him.

He spread both hands out in a placating gesture. "Why do you assume I am here to kill you Cheryl?" he said sounding like he found the idea humorous. "Because that is all your kind have done since I found out about you." I replied confused by his lack of actions. "I am only here as a messenger and an observer. Do you think that all of creation is after you the same? Do you believe that they could possibly all agree on one outcome or one strategy?" he said while folding his hands back into his lap still looking amused. "A messenger from Hell, Yeah I seem to remember what the Bible had to say about them." I replied.

Why wasn't he attacking me? Why just sit there when I could burn him to charcoal from this distance? "Give me your message and go then demon." I said getting angrier at not understanding the situation.

"Allow me to show you something and maybe

you can understand." He said. "Here on this beach? Are you going to show me how the prince of darkness can make the waves bigger or something, oooh scary." I said snarking back. This was the first time I saw anger flash across his face and the demon underneath. "If you insist on using names, it might be best if you used the correct ones. The wrong words and names can bring consequences you will not like." he said with a bite in his voice. "Look" he said and waved a hand in my direction. I suddenly saw in my head several things in rapid succession. A set of throne room's filled with all manner of demons. Some looked like the Scions, some like the worst parts of all manner of beings fused in some grotesque fashion. Still others looked almost Angelic with their beauty. That is when I realized that Juan wasn't like the Scions I had been fighting. He was a different what, race, type? As the image swirled in an upward spiral, The Demons began looking more Angelic but with dark colors instead of the pure white robes associated with cleanliness. I also saw thousands of figures all with very different appearances and all with their particular Demon. I felt a struggle between all of them. It was like invisible lines of support and fighting were drawn between each leader. Showing me who was fighting whom. Then I saw something so beautiful and so twisted at the same time I almost threw up. It left me shaking. I was actually sweating when the images stopped. I couldn't remember a single detail of the last image. For the first time in my life I was grateful to not remember something. I found myself standing in the same place I had been and Juan hadn't moved a muscle.

"What the hell was that?" I asked. "Exactly as you phrased it, Hell and its major players. More specifically, Your hell. In Your heaven, it is black and white, good and bad. On earth it is grayer and in Your hell it is even darker." He said still calm as if we weren't on opposite sides of this. "You will notice there were many thrones in descending order of importance. In Your hell, like your corporate world, everyone wants to take the next throne up from them. They think one more is better and they will be satisfied. There is always one more for them." he said simply.

I had seen this at my old job; the ladder climbers were usually only satisfied with their new position for a short time before wanting their bosses chair. Why wouldn't this be like hell, it made sense. I wanted to ask him why he kept referring to it as "Your hell", Wasn't there only one hell?

"Which throne is yours?" This brought another piece of anger; I could see steam coming from his skin. "Your hell has no place for me, neither does Your heaven. I am content with my place." "Why are you showing me this then? We play for different sides?" I asked. "Because someone is making a power play and using you as their pawn.

How many types of Scions did you see there? How many types have you fought?" he asked. "From what I saw I have only fought two kinds, yeah they fought different but they were basically the same. Are you trying to tell me that you and I aren't enemies?" I asked. "No, we may one day be enemies. One day we might fight each other, but today isn't that day. Today I am here to put a stop to a power play that can't be allowed. It is my duty." He said now reclining into the relaxed posture from before.

"There is a time for everything, but this can't be allowed to continue. Your ArchAngels aren't allowed to interfere with Your hells internal strife even as it affects one of their own players. They can point, but can't tell you if you are supposed to look at the finger pointing or the direction they are pointing in." Isn't that basically what Father Ryan had told me? Something about paths and choice. I tried looking like I wasn't impressed. "A particular demon is your real enemy, the sooner you figure that out the better for you and all of your kind. Look for him, not the Scions you have been maneuvered to fight." he said. It had finality to it. Then I saw why. He vanished, just gone, so was the fire and every sense that the beach had been disturbed at all.

CHAPTER SIXTEEN

I made my way back down the beach somehow. For all I know I might have teleported. I was so trapped in my own thoughts, the beach, waves, and people blurred into background noise. The Scions could have jumped me and cut me to ribbons before I knew what hit me. Thankfully they stayed away for now. Except for Juan, Nothing from the other side seemed to be within a hundred miles. I couldn't even sense Juan anymore, though I didn't notice him before I was close enough for him to kill me earlier. I tried to focus, but every thought led to more questions. Why Juan referred to everything as "Your hell, Your heaven, Your, Your, Your." Was everything I dealt with personal to me? Is that how hell worked? Is that how faith worked? Grasping something so fractured and individualized would be more difficult than a thousand books could explain.

Until now I had operated as if they were all individual groups. How could I not see them as a collective whole? "Because, you were supposed to see them that way." I answered myself. I somehow found myself in a bubble bath I don't remember drawing. What was that saying about madness? Talking to yourself wasn't crazy, but if you started answering yourself.

I tried to stay focused on the problem at hand. My own sanity could wait for further dissection later. So were each group the trap, or were they more like hunting dogs trying to tree the prey? Both scenarios made sense. If one of the groups happened to kill me then that was fine, the end goal was the same. Eliminate the last Sprite before she could become a problem. Crap.

I was clean and sitting on the bed, the weather was a little chilly outside and it was so beautiful. I knew I felt safe here, but I couldn't be sure. At least I could pick the tree they tried to make me climb. As beautiful as this place was, it didn't make for an ideal fighting position. If I get trapped in here, the ocean cuts me off from one route of escape. Was that why I felt compelled to get to an island during the first run-in with them? They made me feel like fleeing somewhere that only had one entrance, but also only one exit. It forced me to fight.

I needed options, I needed somewhere they wouldn't have the advantage. I puzzled over how to take their speed and turn it against them. I pulled out my phone. "Search, Belial" I said clearly into it. I hoped I pronounced it right. I don't know where that name came from but it felt right. Wow that was a lot of information. After the tenth page the thing that stood out the most was Prince of Lies. Great, whatever I was dealing with was a super liar. This was as helpful to me figuring this out, as learning he was male but could appear female.

I took a steadying breath then made a plan. I had everything packed and ready to go in less than thirty minutes. In less than an hour I was ready to hit the road. That was when I sensed Scions nearby. Not just a group of them, A lot of them. I have no idea how I knew this, but something in me was sure that a freaking army of Scions were descending on my paradise. I dropped the key for my room in the night deposit slot and got on the interstate as fast as possible. I could still sense them but they seemed to be heading away from me, still towards the room on the beach. I drove faster than I thought my little mini could handle. Thankfully at this time of the night there weren't many cars on the road. Even more thankfully I seemed to know when to slow down for speed traps.

CHAPTER SEVENTEEN

I drove for three days, only stopping for gas and quick rest breaks. I was so tired by the time I hit the Tennessee border that I knew if I didn't stop acting like a rabbit, I was going to wear myself out. I didn't want it to be Tennessee because I shouldn't stop somewhere I've been before. It also meant I was close enough to visit my mom and friends. I couldn't put my finger on how I knew that was a bad idea.

I already knew the group chasing me had good intelligence about my life and would know where I felt safe. In spite of all this, I had to stop or I was going to fall asleep on the road. I am pretty sure that hitting a tree at eighty would end my trip as much as their claws could. Tennessee in August, good choice. It was the middle of the night, I am pretty sure it was in the nineties with one hundred percent humidity. My back and legs were stuck to the seats of the car. Even with the air conditioning running at full blast, it was sticky with the moisture in the air.

Before stopping, I reached out to see if they were anywhere near, not even a blip. I hadn't felt them since I hit Arizona. I went the wrong way in Dallas when I hit that mess of interstates converging. I was almost in Utah before I realized my mistake. Now I just had to find somewhere to sleep that wouldn't ask too many questions.

I didn't know how they were tracking me, but

if it was through the mundane use of bank cards, I had them fooled. I stopped using those when the money in the accounts dried up six months ago. That must not have been the only way they tracked me, though, it might have been one of the ways. Who says demons can't use Google. No, I bet they still used AOL.

My room was far enough from the highway to give me a cushion. If they came in that way I had plenty of chances to escape before they got too close. I could track them at longer distances now. I am not sure if that was due to training in the line of fire, or a natural increase in my abilities. I could definitely cook them easier. With the walking stick... Crap, I left the walking stick in the room behind the door in California.

Somehow, I doubt they were considerate enough to pick it up for me while they were there. A laugh slipped from me as I imagined one of them bowing, handing me the walking stick "You may smite us now ma lady." yeah that wasn't going to happen, though the idea made me laugh harder. Maybe I was getting slap happy. Without the staff I was back to just my fire, which had proved ineffective against several of the groups. When I had it with me I could use the lightning, hail, and wind to disrupt them too. How could I have forgotten it while being chased by the things it was made for destroying?

I lay in bed trying to quiet my mind enough for

some sleep. Just as I was about to fall asleep, it occurred to me. Before the walking stick came into my possession, I had random encounters with them. After I had it they seemed to be chasing me non-stop. I knew the staff was a force for good, but what if they could use it like a homing beacon. If they could sense it like I could sense them, then I wasn't safe around it. I pictured some faceless bad guy screaming no in a dramatic movie scene. There was that giggle again. Dang I am a nerd. That was what I needed, because the next thing I knew housekeeping was knocking.

I tipped her as I left the room to look around for little things I would need. I found some lunch, and came back. I paid the desk guy for another night and went to my room to eat. My car was parked in the middle of a long line of cars so it would be hard to spot unless you were on top of it.

I knew I needed answers and not just from the other side of the fence. I needed someone on my side who knew what was going on. I know that the ArchAngels were out. They couldn't influence me so it would be like holding a conversation with a cat. That is, of course, if they would show up at all. I needed my own intermediary. I wasn't sure how to call him so I just did what I had before. Picturing Father Ryan in my head. His balding head, his blue eyes, and his devilish smile. It only took a few minutes. I was all alone in the room then he was there. "Good evening Angel." he said with a broad grin. "I thought I lost you."

CHAPTER EIGHTEEN

At first Father Ryan didn't say anything; he just smiled and walked around the small room. I asked again "Why haven't the Scions shown their ugly heads yet?" He smiled back at me as he sat down again. "I see you gave up the Rod of Moses. Why?" Something in his tone wasn't quite a question. It was more of disbelief. "Rod of Moses? Do you mean the walking stick? Sure it was awesome, but not worth my life to go back for with hell coming for me." This wasn't even a question, I didn't care whose stick, rod, staff, or other phallic reference it was, it wasn't worth my life to go back to get. I would have gone back for my favorite Chuck Taylor's at my house had that been the case. It was just stuff, if I wasn't alive to enjoy it, then it wasn't very valuable at that point.

Father Ryan steepled his fingers in thought and didn't say anything, "You do realize it gave you access to powers you wouldn't haven't mastered yet to fight back. The Scions may be marshaling their forces, or they may be planning a different sort of assault. I do know they don't get along very well outside of their parent groups unless ordered to do so. You need to remember that they are your opposite and equal. For every bit of love you have, they contain hate, for every piece of compassion you may contain they only have hunger. They are the cast out, the unworthy, the unclean, and they will never forget it. You might do well to remember that too. Nothing any of them says to you can be counted as truth; they even lie to each other." He finished.

I thought this last part was referring to what Juan the demon guy told me. I was so confused. Had Juan only shown me a little of what was truly there? Was there something important he omitted. Now I had an idea who one of my adversaries were and why only two kinds of Scion were after me. I was about to ask Father Ryan about them but for some reason I couldn't say Belial out loud. I couldn't make the sentence come out right. So I just stayed quiet.

Father Ryan didn't stay for long after that, sitting in uncomfortable silence. He did warn me that some of the groups would be getting close soon and I should find a safe place to fight them because running wasn't going to work forever with so many active groups. Hadn't Juan said this was a power play.

Everything I had read and more importantly felt, told me that was right. A power play was perfectly in line with the nature of hell itself. Beings so filled with all the sins, like coveting, would never be satisfied with their station. I tried to reason out the logic, I left the staff or rod or whatever of Moses. How could I have missed it? I thought back to the terror filled moments of fleeing. I can't remember seeing it there by the door where it should have been. Had it been there, I would have grabbed it on the way out. Maybe I was remembering it wrong. In my haste I just missed it.

There were twenty four Scions after me from a long way off. How did I suddenly know how many were after me. At the time I just thought it was half of hell coming for me, but now when I thought about it I was sure it had been exactly twenty four. I lay down on the cheap crappy bed of the no tell motel. I am sure it was bad enough I could find someone cooking meth in the next room if I cared to look.

I don't remember falling asleep but I was exhausted after everything and must have dozed off again. I woke up thirty minutes later filled with terror. Something was close, four something's. What happened to the other twenty? I wasn't complaining, four were easier than twenty four, still the question stuck in my mind. I jumped up and went outside of the room with two steps. Did I mention how tiny the rooms were? I could tell there was something in the woods just outside the hotel parking lot. I looked down at my car, my only way of getting around. I wasn't getting stuck here. I made a stupid decision and ran down the stairs and strode into the woods to meet them head on. I wasn't running from four punk ass Scions.

It had to be close to midnight and a new moon as dark as it was in the woods. I kept listening for any approach, claws on the dirt, the charging and horrible beating sound they seemed to make when excited by the hunt. There was nothing, not a single sound. The air was thick, from the heat and the humidity, but there was something else. No bats, no night birds, no rodents. That was a good sign they were here, but it felt like there was a clear ring around me like they were standing just outside of it in perfect symmetry.

Then I felt it, pressure, like the circle was closing I couldn't sense anything outside of it. I was being contained. I had never been cut off from the outside world but, if I let them choose when and how to attack I was at their mercy. I picked a side at random. Then I sprinted toward it as fast as I could to meet one of them head on before they had time to prepare whatever they were going to do. I could feel the edge of the circle getting close and got ready to fight. I reached the edge and nothing. There was nothing there, just a break in the pressure. I could feel one close by, but couldn't see them anywhere. I had already dealt with ones that could disappear and reappear, but that was over short distances. That wasn't complete invisibility. I looked around as I felt the others getting closer.

I could feel it was a male, I could feel he was right here, but I couldn't see him. If he was that close, why hadn't he attacked. Far off I felt a fifth presence but it was different. It wasn't a Scion but it was twice as nauseating. I knew it was the old white haired Demon I saw when I was being attacked by the cactus looking Scions. I spun to face the way the ones getting closer were coming from. I couldn't see anything at all. I heard the tree sway at the last second. By the time I looked up all four were on their way down with gravity accelerating them, all claws and teeth.

They climbed in through the trees. Instead of fighting they were planning an ambush. They wanted this over; I hadn't seen them as more than mindless killing machines before now. Strategy wasn't their forte. I dodged and rolled, then I almost let myself get distracted by the stronger presence from the fifth thing.

All four attacked like a single unit. What the hell were they suddenly ninjas? Something wasn't right. I caught one out of the edge of the charging group with a fire and wind burst, holy crap; I could still do the wind thing. The other three didn't even flinch as they sprinted at me. In the split second I was preparing another burst to cut them down to two, then I noticed they didn't have white hair on their head but black spikes covering their chit nous bodies.

I knew when they showed up it meant something, even as I blew another one into a tree. The remaining two, one female, one male came toward me. They started to break ranks just slightly, dammit; I was going to try and get them both with one big burst and use their spikes against each other. They weren't a matched pair. I knew they weren't, I had fried their companions on my first two bursts. Great now they were pissed and still working together. I jumped as one went for my knees with his claws. But the female caught me across the stomach while I was in the air with one of her spikes.

Oh God that hurt. My skin was burning from the cut, she got me good. The male grabbed both of my legs and pulled. I went into full panic mode; I nearly froze in place for some stupid reason. Then everything rushed back into real-time and I swung down with both hands and caught the male on his head and put everything into one big burst. I knew if I got it down to one it would be easier to fight. I hit him square in the head as I started getting dizzy from all the power I just sent out, and from the blood loss. My stomach wasn't going to be pretty and my jeans were soaking through with blood. The one that grabbed my legs erupted into flames with his entire head going at once. These Scions could be burnt; it just took a lot more fire power to get them started. I hit the ground and my legs gave out. I was shaking in a way that had nothing to do with the temperature. I was done, collapsed, bleeding, and there was still one left. I can't believe I got myself into this by charging head first. I remember thinking my poor car would end up impounded, or worse in the hands of that nasty desk clerk when I didn't come back, I remember thinking how the two dark spots in my vision seemed to blur into a haze. I could feel the female charging in to finish the job. Why did I leave the walking stick? That would have made the difference.

CHAPTER NINETEEN

I guess I never stopped long enough to think about what happens to a Sprite that is killed. Do we automatically go to heaven, hell, nowhere? You'll have to cut me some slack, before I learned I was a Sprite I was one hundred percent scientist about it all. I sure didn't think of Alice in Wonderland scenery. Everything around me that shouldn't have been alive and sentient was, and way too much so. The plants bent to watch me walk past on the path that moved of its own accord.

I'm not sure why I stayed on the path. There were green fields on either side now with distant tree lines. Places to run, do cartwheels, roll in the grass, pretty much anything I wanted. I followed the moving path. It was like trying to walk on the back of a moving snake. I had to calculate every footstep before I took it to make sure the path would be under it. I became so consumed with this I forgot to pay attention to where it was going. I know the whole "The journey is what really matters" thing; they never mention moving roads that try to trip you up by turning at the last minute. Maybe I read Alice too much as a kid, or watched the Wizard of Oz with the scary Poppy scene; I just knew I wasn't stepping off this path no matter what. I felt something dark to my right. I tried to scan for it but it was in the tree lines. At first, I told myself I had plenty of time to react if it broke cover, then I realized physical distance didn't seem to be the same obstacle it was on Earth. I turned and looked at where I had started an hour ago. It looked like two steps away. But I was right in the middle of the field, the empty field. The walking to nowhere was going to get boring fast. I felt the dark presence moving faster on my right. I knew it was in the trees this time, "Hell of a time to learn to use it in three dimensions now" I said out loud to myself. No reason to keep my inner dialogue stuck in my head. It was refreshing to say these things out loud anyway.

"So, this is what I had to look forward too? Not even killer flowers to take me out for going the wrong way?" I said thinking again of my childhood favorites. "I wouldn't quite put it that way." a strong timbre came from behind me, even the grass seemed to bend away from the voice. I spun ready to fight what I had been sensing, how had it snuck up on me when I was so aware of its location? When I looked I only saw legs, white legs, I looked up slowly. "Oh God, you're naked. Decency much?" I heard a boom and the ground shook. I steadied myself and looked back up. The man was my size now and still not wearing pants. He was white almost to the point of being alabaster, little ringlets of hair spun down in ways I could never get mine to do with the best tools and hair product. He had a lean face with the required high cheekbones of every Greek god I ever saw depicted. His eyes were a blazing blue, not like human blue, like the fire that came from my fists blue. His nose couldn't have been more defined if someone took a chisel to marble. I couldn't shake the idea of talking to a living statue.

"Poor choice of words child." It came out almost like a laugh. "You will find this is not the place to use such...Colorful expressions", He said. I wasn't sure exactly what was going on, I could hear his words perfectly well and yet I could see them and feel them too. They were a living creature of their own. I couldn't help it, I wondered if he said unicorn, one would simply appear. We both heard it at the same time. A brilliant white unicorn with silver laced mane and tail, opalescent horn, and beautiful unmarred white fur covering him. It was eating grass and not even noticing our presence. The man smiled, then waved a hand as the unicorn just unmade, I don't mean disappeared but sunk back into the grass like he had always been part of it. "A beautiful idea child, but this is not his time. You have worked out that the flames of creation are yours to command, it is what you do with them that matters. You owe your existence to important words." he finished in a more regal manner than I am sure all the kings of England ever commanded. "Yes I have read the whole Genesis section and" he stopped me there. Not with the words, just the will behind the words, "You Do not understand my meaning child. Allow me to show you."

The landscape blurred and I could see my mom, holy crap she looked great. She was sitting on a school quad at college. Her long red hair draped around her like armor. Even her body language said "back off." Several shirtless boys showing off nearby throwing a Frisbee and catching it in unique and acrobatic ways. She kept her head down better than I would have managed. They were kind of hot. She kept reading her book. While sitting in a white, almost see through flowery skirt and matching top. Then a boy with reddish cheeks, brown short hair and a too tight t-shirt walked up and sat next to her. She didn't pay him any attention at all, even as he sat uncomfortably close. He leaned in pretending to read over her shoulder and whispered something to her. I am not sure how but, I knew but that was it for her. That was the one. Was that my dad? All of my pictures of him where ruined in a fire when I was young and I couldn't remember him. I was too young when he died. Mom looked happier than I had ever seen her before. Then the boy got up and walked away. Each step taking him further away but my mom kept looking forward smiling. I turned to look and the boy was gone.

I looked at the man with me, "What the He... Heck was that" I corrected myself. "That was your conception child." he replied with the same force as before. "No, no, no, no, My mom was married in Bakersfield, Her and my dad raised me until he died in a car wreck. Then we moved to Tennessee and never left. She even has some of his stuff." I said. I hadn't realized I was physically backing away from him at the same time. That was, until he yelled. No, his mouth didn't move, he thought "STOP." I forced my feet to quit backpedaling. Looking down, I realized I was right on the edge of the path and near the woods. He was still only a few steps away, but it seemed like the whole distance shrunk proportionally. "Ask yourself child, what is a concept?" he asked placing both hands out like he wanted to know what two plus two was from a small kid.

"An idea." I answered like it was a university question. "Yes and No." he said sounding more like my Physics professor than he should have. "An idea is nothing until it is shared. A concept is an idea, a thought, a creation of will shared between people." "So you're saying conception is the act of sharing an idea, I think you missed the human anatomy course." I replied before I could stop myself. I didn't know who this was, or who he was supposed to be and probably shouldn't mouth off to someone so powerful he was capable of changing the landscape with just a thought. "No child, I don't believe I missed anything ever." As pompous as this would normally sound from anyone else, I had a feeling he meant it and was right. "So you're saying my dad never existed?" I replied a little more hotly than I should have. I was always protective of any mention of my dad. Something left over from my childhood, when I was teased about not having a dad. Kids today lived with American flags folded over mantles instead of fathers and mothers all over the country. I bet no one was dumb enough to tease them.

The man waited patiently for my internal rant to cease before answering. "Your dad was as real as anything in this world, God's words; my sharing them gave him breath and gave you life inside your mother. All of the memories are still there, all of the feelings, the love, the heartache, his death. Do you not feel stirrings of his memory in your own heart?" he finished. "Whoa, wait a minute, are you saying you helped make me? I buy the whole demons are real, or something like them, I have seen hell, I think I have seen heaven now, but you are NOT MY DAD." I finished breathing harder than I should have been. He chuckled, a rumbling laugh. It was deep and shook everything even the distant trees that had receded, though I hadn't moved since backpedaling. "Not quite child, are you familiar with the Seraphim and the great flood GOD sent to cleanse the world of them and their horrific battles?" Even in his speech I could hear the all caps he put on God. "Yeah the story of Noah right? But if I am not half-human half-Angel and I sure as heck am not God's forgotten daughter to his better known son, what am I?" I asked trying to puzzle it out.

I knew better than to believe I was vanilla mortal anymore. I had seen sci-fi movies that weren't as far-fetched. "That is an IMPORTANT question." He said again with the all caps thing. "So I am not a Seraphim, I am not the female Jesus, but I am not purely mortal." I puzzled to myself out loud. I thumped my head with my hand. A bad habit from late nights studying at University. It just wouldn't come, It was like knowing there had to be a fourth answer on the test but someone left it blank by accident and you knew the other three answers were wrong. "Did you do something like this to my mom again so she wouldn't miss me?" it was a straight forward question. I noticed a hesitance that hadn't been there before. Something he wasn't telling me.

"Your mother sees what she wants to see. It didn't take a visit to let her still feel you were in her heart." I started getting angry again. I hated being lied to; I hated the evasive answers even more. "It is a yes or no question; does my mom think I am still there?" The ArchAngel dipped his head slightly, then he followed the movement with a quiet "yes" I wanted to rage, I wanted to vent and yell. Every piece of anger just slipped away instead. I was numb everywhere the adrenaline had been before. I began to open my mouth anyway. I had no words. Without the anger behind them, they just wouldn't come out.

You were created to stop the liar." I took this in as he said it. "Oh you mean Beli...." my voice stopped working. I was breathing, my lips moved, nothing came out. "You never speak that, even his name is his power, for it is a lie as well. He cannot know you are here now." I nodded and my voice came back. I settled for an "OK." and left it at that. That was safe to say right? "Now it is time for you to venture back the way you came. You will find new strength from your understanding. Use it carefully; there are still dark plans that can unmake you." I had questions but knew that was the last thing he would say to me, at least for now." I turned my head, and the way I came in looked like a door just a step away. I inhaled hard and held it like I was jumping from a high dive and pushed through.

I was on my back, the leaves were slimy under my back from my blood and that bitch was almost on top of me. I threw both hands out and smiled. A fireball the size of my car flew straight into her. She didn't just turn to ash, or catch fire. She was gone, I mean completely erased. I felt around, nothing in the trees, the figure I had felt earlier was gone as well. My stomach was still thrashed and it left me feeling light headed. It took forever to get myself to a seated position. I remembered the whole frailties part of the speech. That part was too clear. Somehow I got myself to my feet. I don't remember much after that. I woke up in the no tell meth hotel. I could see my stomach wounds puckered and red, a little oozing, but pieces of duct tape were holding it closed. That was going to seriously hurt when it came time to take it off.

CHAPTER TWENTY

So that happened, and yeah the duct tape hurt like hell to remove. At least I had some good battle scars that every girl loves come bikini season. I managed to duck in and out of cover while I studied furiously trying to find any hints of the things that ArchAngel had told me. I fought off the urge to call my mom again. He may have been able to keep me from raging out on him but that didn't make it hurt less to think of my mom carrying on as if I was still there. I had to get my mind on something else.

I still wondered which ArchAngel it was. A ton of research later and I had it narrowed down to two. Uriel, He was the sneaky one who did all the dirty work, and Metatron the chatty one. I know that wasn't how the Bible and other religious texts described them, it was just sort of the feeling I came away with. An ArchAngel willing to actually speak to me didn't seem like something they could decide to do on their own. Uriel seemed to always be the unknown quantity. If there was something difficult to deal with or even remotely underhanded, it seemed to fall on him. I was leaning toward Uriel, because making an end run around the "no more Seraphim" rule wasn't tracking with the others that were actually mentioned. More importantly I noted how many were mentioned but never named.

I have always been too smart for my own good,

but the information I received in August as well as the new upgrade in powers kept me baffled. I understood I was like a wish fulfillment, but did that mean my mom looked crazy six months pregnant walking around a Kroger talking to someone that was only in her mind, or did others see my not-father and never question it. I wanted to call her and ask for more information but I am sure the ArchAngel, or God himself did a perfect job to convince the super skeptic that my not-dad was real and I was still there. I had no idea if it also meant I was immortal, or just really powerful. Like Bruce Lee's nun-chucks, ordinary in any other hands but could be devastating when he used them. I know I am over-thinking this but it is kind of what I do. Maybe it just was, and I was meant to do what I could to make the world a better place. Like a superhero with a very select group of bad guys I could fight.

I tried to stop a robbery at a convenience store near my new trailer home but ended up just looking like I was having a seizure lying on the floor moving my hands around at the gunman. He probably just thought I was deaf and signing to him instead of trying to incinerate him.

I practiced every day for my next fight, oh and I ran a lot. Just in case, you know, because the whole he who lives to fight blah blah blah. I tried to call Father Ryan several times for counsel, questions, comfort, and anything else to help.

Guess that link was cut for some reason too. I hadn't seen him since that night just before the fight in Tennessee near that horrid hotel. I also hadn't seen or felt the twenty other scions I felt months ago. He probably only showed up when I was about to be killed or something.

I tried looking up more about the rod or staff of Moses, but didn't find out much more than I already knew. It helped him call down all kinds of freaky weather to protect his people in great times of danger, turned to snakes in the presence of the pharaoh, and helped Moses with his many wonders leading his people from slavery. I thought it was interesting that I was fighting all the time while I had it and nothing at all for months when I left it behind. I tried to put the pieces together but the best I had come up with was, it somehow invited challenges, or the demons could track it because it was so powerful and old. There was so much to process. I tried my best to keep my thoughts to what I knew versus wild guesses.

The first days back had been full of the what-ifs and they didn't lead me anywhere. Just self-doubt, you know like was I crazy, did someone slip me LSD at a party and I was one of those stories you hear about the permanent trip where the person never comes down. That did have the convenience of a lack of sleep. Since coming back from the almost dead, sleep was a lucky accident.

It was incredibly boring, and lonely. I only left the trailer long enough to get supplies and the occasional visit to the goodwill for clothes. I was still in Tennessee, but in a very rural part of it. I was running out of money though and probably wouldn't be able to make it a few more months here without some kind of miracle. I thought about the demon boy I kissed, was that really so long ago? I tried to date a few times before all of this but they all ended worse than if I had been dating demon boy Juan. At least I knew what his motivations were. I think. He made no apologies for what he was, he just was. Why couldn't people be like that?

I swear I thought about him for only a second, the feel of his lips on mine near that fire, just before the whole slithery feeling thing. Was I losing it thinking romantically about a freaking demon? I didn't even know what kind of demon he was, he never said. Was he a cast out Angel, a bad man who died and managed to ladder climb his way in hell too. The son of some horrible union, like a reverse Seraphim or whatever that would be called.

Before I knew it my thoughts were full of questions about him. Maybe he some ancient Aztec that killed millions for a crazy sky deity, or crazed warlord controlling an entire country before someone stepped in to stop him. I didn't fool myself into thinking he was human by any means. He would have never become this powerful if he hadn't been something truly evil before. I mean he was the freaking enemy. I shouldn't have thought about him other than wanting to kill him like the bitch that jumped me in the woods.

I felt it before I saw him there. He appeared like Father Ryan had. Just there, like he had been sitting there the whole time and waiting for me to look at him. I half jumped and prepared a fire blast in his direction before I even looked. I saw the look in Juan's eyes and his half grin. The fire died before I could throw it. Like the fire knew I didn't mean it.

"How are you doing Cheryl? Any luck with Belial? He really has been in a temper lately, so you must have done something right." He said slowly but confident in every word. "Why do you think it was me? Maybe he pissed off someone bigger." I replied feeling sheepish that I actually was capable of creating any inconvenience to one of hell's soldiers. I was a freaking office drone without an office. "Oh, it is definitely you. He was tracking you just fine while you had the bane rod, now he has no more bead on you than he did before you came into possession of it. I doubt he would still be around if you still had it, you would have eliminated him already. He is just too prideful to admit it." He said simply. I laughed, harder than I should have. "So your telling me a cute redhead has him running? He doesn't sound like much of a threat that way." Juan's face grew dark at my poor attempt at a joke. "You may not appreciate what you are to the world or to its future, but yes he has good reason to be afraid of you." he said. He didn't miss a beat and resumed before I could laugh again. "You have seen your progenitor, you have followed the path to your heaven and returned stronger for it. He doesn't know how you are more powerful, and I am not in the sharing mood at the moment. He is scared to continue his plan when you have destroyed what the others couldn't." he finished as if he was done explaining.

 "What put you in such a strong position down there? Where you some kind of evil here before you died or just an original Angel cast down?" I couldn't have poured ice water on him and got more of a reaction. His pleasant face broke; he was so close I could only see his eyes with the wall keeping me from moving any further back. "You will not understand, I will never be perfect but I know my place Cheryl, you need to remember yours. I will not answer for the position put upon me. I may not have had a choice but at least I own it. What have you done with yours?" I couldn't breathe to answer. I wanted him away from me, no one treated me like that and didn't get something in return. I had to get him away from me, then Juan was flying out of the room and through the outer wall of the trailer with a gust of wind coming from every bit of my body, I fell to the floor in the now empty room. "He is coming with all he has, be prepared Cheryl. I hope we do a fine battle one day, don't think of me again." echoed Juan's voice.

Before I could register what just happened I could feel it like an earthquake. The footfalls of twenty-four of the most evil things I had ever felt. Shit, I couldn't get out fast enough. Twenty-four to one was really unfair. What the hell, I pissed off my demon boy and had no other prospects in mind so this day just gave me the gift of fighting back. I stepped on the stoop outside the trailer. Just in time to see the neighbor's door burst open scraping ice away as it moved

CHAPTER TWENTY-ONE

If my heart could beat faster than it was right now, I am sure a doctor would have me in for observations. I could hear a thunderous roar in the distance, trees snapping as giant arms ripped through broken branches. I looked over at my scumbag neighbor, he looked one step from homeless with his raggedy black pea coat, his over-sized paint splattered pants, and his crazy half boot shoes. Now that I looked at him he was probably good looking under all that grime and paint. I was curious what color hair he had, I don't know why, he always wore a hat that covered it completely. I had more pressing matters to deal with anyway.

Distraction, that should have been my name. The fact that he could hear the Scions too was saying something about the lack of stealth they were employing. I looked to the woods.

I knew the woods really well now; I knew where there were hides, and creeks, as well as low branches of ancient trees reaching out like hands. I grabbed my coat and shoes and sprinted out to keep the battle away from people who might get hurt. They might use innocent casualties to distract me. I ran past the parking lot and into the tree line. I followed my normal running path since it seemed to intersect nicely with the direction I felt them. I had a branch I made into a staff for fighting since the loss of Moses' rod. I had six years of study fighting with a staff and it felt normal to me. Magically imbued by God or not, I knew I could use it effectively. I used it as a walking stick steadying my run right now. The ground was frozen in places where the trees were thinner and many of the branches I usually ran under without a problem were sagging under the weight of ice. I got to the clearing first and turned to wait for them.

The first group arrived, four of them, their shock white hair, crystal blue eyes and bands of sinew. They were fast, feral, and deadly. They had either given up the disguise outer shells, or I just couldn't see those anymore. I couldn't be sure, but it really didn't matter now. Before I could even lift the staff from the ground to a fighting stance, one of them dove for me, a male that had at least a hundred pounds of black sinew worth of weight on me. He was heading straight at my center of mass with his claws extended. He only dropped a fraction of an inch in the fifty feet he flew; the jump had to be a new Olympic record. I put my weight on the staff and spun clockwise like it was the pivot on a carousel. The Scion reached out the claws on his hand to snatch at me as he flew by, it struck my staff instead. I figured I was going to be fighting with a stick instead of a staff now, but his claws shattered on impact. It should have sliced it into pieces; I saw one gouge the roof of my car with only the effort of slowing herself down.

Claws met the wood, and just shattered like they were made of ice. He tucked his wounded hand in and rolled into a defensive position thirty feet past me. What a good time for them to read "The Art of War" and plan a divisive strategy. With him on that side and the other three on the opposite, I couldn't do more than turn to keep them all in my peripheral vision. If they realized this and went to a more defensible approach I was dead. I tried to discourage any other change by charging him. I knew this left the other three to attack my rear flank but they would have ground to cover first and I doubt they all could make the leap he did. If so the fight was over already.

He lunged at me when I was within striking distance with his left arm. It was an upward swing meant to eviscerate me, but I met it low with a strike from the staff and spun it into a head shot in the same motion. His arm dropped to the ground and looked like it was lamed as well and my head shot had the desired effect. He fell to the right of me when the next one dove for me. Instead of spinning to defend myself, I tucked and rolled out of the way and sprung back to my feet. I came up in time to see him try to correct his course but too late, for all their power, physics still mattered. He struck the wounded one full on at top speed. It was like watching a car wreck, you knew it wasn't going to end well but you had to see it happen. The stationary one with the arm wounds bore most of the brunt in his upper body and it launched him like a missile into the old oak tree behind him. He hit with such force that, had it been any less of a tree, it might have broken. Instead I saw a shock-wave travel through his black mass like jelly. I don't know if the demons have insides to liquefy but he dropped just as effectively. No twitch, no bounce, just the thud of him hitting and the crack of the frozen ground underneath. The other tumbled to the left and didn't jump right back up. Shit, I let the females get too close behind me. I spun the staff up in a backward jousting motion and caught one of them obliquely on the shoulder spinning her out of her mid leap. The other managed to slip past and shredded the back of my shirt and pants leaving fresh gashes where she struck. She tucked and rolled gracefully after the attack springing to her feet. The one I spun out of control jumped back up. This felt familiar, one on each side, then I felt my body flying backwards, with a linebacker charge from the male that had tumbled off kilter earlier. I didn't even see him get back up. Before I hit the ground I planted the staff in the ground and used it like a pole-vaulter, sending me further back and letting his momentum carry me further away instead of taking all the impact myself.

My hands were burning; I would have blisters for sure. I glanced down in time to see my hands were literally on fire, and so was the staff. It wasn't charring. It wasn't smoking. As a matter of fact, it was perfectly intact under the blue-white flames. I spun it through the air and struck the one who had just tackled me, he tried to roll out of the way but wasn't fast enough. The moment my staff hit him, his shoulder burst into flames. He was beating on it like a Boy Scout fire drill. I took the distraction to strike him with ten quick strikes. None of them alone would hurt him physically, but the resulting impact of all of them in less than a few seconds along with the fires they started made sure he wouldn't get back up again. He was less than ashes. I looked up at the others and saw shock in their eye's. They both broke formation and charged me mindlessly. Fight or flight, I guess even Scions weren't immune to that. Charging like that was what I hoped from them. I incinerated one with my right hand as she reached me and struck the other with the staff in my left hand on her head, shoulder and hip. I spun to see the aftermath of the staff strikes; it was more like I had hit her with a sword. The staff had carved her into pieces. Each part its own little blue-white fire pit. I calmly walked over to the limp form of the first one. I could feel the blood running down my back and was having trouble keeping my pants up with part of the back slashed just across my butt. I got to him and drove the staff down into his still limp form right in the place a heart should have been. I watched as the flames ran out to cover his whole body.

I heard more rustling and a growl behind me. I turned to the growl, my pants fell down, I tried to pull them back up. Even with the adrenaline, it was cold. They shouldn't have dropped all the way to my knees; they took forever to pour myself into. I tried to get them back up. I wasn't going to die from hypothermia fighting in my panties and a partially ruined coat. I also couldn't fight it with my legs bound at the knees by my jeans. My decision was cut short as something the size of a freaking house came through the tree line. He was a twenty foot tall version of the ones that had attacked me in August. Black spikes jutting out everywhere just daring me to touch one of them. Each leg was my height alone. "This better work." I said as I struck my staff down between my legs. The jeans split right through the middle leaving me with denim leg warmers instead of pants, orange panties, and a torn red coat. The giant Scion took one more step toward me. I should have screamed but, I had no fear left in me, just a pit of anger and fire. Either way this ended here somehow. I already made a battle plan in my head. Dear lord I hope this works.

CHAPTER TWENTY-TWO

Something was off, the huge monster hulking before me looked like a big Scion, but felt like twenty Scions. It was a MegaScion. Regular spiked Scions formed the disjointed limbs and individual portions of body. I was already beginning to shiver with the cold, dressed in my heavy coat, but practically naked from the waist down. The blue jean leggings protecting my lower legs from the bite of the winter wind but soaked through with ice and snow. Not much material to cover the rest of my lower body though. My staff still held in my hands and glowing, but putting off too little heat to really help. I could feel the presence behind the monster as well. Like an energy source binding them together and giving them directions. Before I could take in more, the first charge began.

He may have been large and powerful, but he wasn't as agile as the smaller ones he was made from. I bounded out of the way. Trying a strike at him with my staff. Flames still flickering down its length. I struck the left leg Scion across the kneecap and watched for the flames to erupt where it struck or a cut of some kind. Instead of the usual crunch, or even the meaty sound of a flesh yielding to the impact, the staff rebounded in my hand like a mishit baseball bat. Vibrations down both arms transferring from the strike. A tiny flicker of flame transferred to the leg and extinguished. It took all my strength to not drop the staff; I spun further out of the way. The roll having deposited snow on my bare legs adding to the feel of the cold wind on my skin. My hands numb from the shock began to flicker feebly with the fire that previously engulfed them. I was done; I couldn't keep fighting this thing. I also knew there was no way it would let me get away. It was standing directly between me and the car park. There was still the presence behind me. It was stronger than the behemoth in front of me.

The MegaScion spoke as it climbed back to its feet. "Amon has determined you gone from this world little Sprite. You will be dispatched. Put down your new bane and accept your fate. Continuing to fight will only draw the inevitable out more." His voice was creepy. Deep as you would expect but sounding like a chorus amplified instead of a single deep resonance. "You won't find me so easy to kill, ask your brothers and sisters in a few moments." I said hoping to draw him into another charge clearing my path. Something was holding him there though. I could see him urging to attack, He might be a MegaScion, but I knew the twenty Scion brains from each piece of him were pushing for an attack. I was dimly aware of a line. It wasn't a physical line but a line anyway. It traveled back to the other presence. I could feel the band of energy traveling from MegaScion to the other presence.

So, he is being controlled at a distance, by a powerful puppet sting. Maybe I could make like a pair of scissors and cut the string. Then I would be able to cut it off from its controller. A giant hand swiped for me and I rolled out of the way of the claws just in time. My legs had gone from a tingling cold to an almost burning sensation anywhere the snow was touching. The ice began burning my skin. My legs hurt so bad, I knew the next step was the loss of feeling and that would be worse in the long run. My knees creaked from the cold. The MegaScion roared at missing me again but still held in place. He was well within striking range but I needed him to shift just a little so I could get to the dark line of energy controlling him. "Are you the biggest, baddest, monkey they can throw at me? Because from where I am standing you look like you're just a puppy on a leash." Before he could make another swipe he finally shifted enough, I grabbed the staff with both hands and struck the still night air in a slashing motion. I imagined using the staff as a sword cleaving the invisible strings connecting him with his source.

Fire erupted from midair and shot down both directions. It was like lighting the middle of a fuse. The flames traveled at a tremendous speed away from each other. One flying out to the middle of the woods, the other directly into the chest of the MegaScion. It did what I hoped. It struck the MegaScion off his feet and threw him like a baseball backwards. I couldn't tell the effect on the other end because the presence there was just gone. I would count that in the plus column. The MegaScion went through three trees in rapid succession splintering them like a cannonball. Each impact spun a part of his body off. His hand and forearm spun off in an odd angle. Individual Scions stretching and popping as it struck the second tree and a leg came loose. I started back toward the car when the presence formed a semicircle around me, I could still sense all twenty Scions individually now.

Crap, what had I done? They were spread out fanning me and charging. I turned and ran. I ducked and leapt over the uneven terrain. They weren't a single entity now; they were twenty Sprite thirsty Scions. I had a good idea of the hazards after running out here daily for months. I cleared the ice covered creek in one solid leap. I tried to keep ahead of them, but I could tell all of them were closing fast. I had to get away from them. One slipped on a patch of ice that had been a large puddle a few days ago, slowing his chase. He tried to regain his footing, I guess even with claws ice can suck. I started feeling the semicircle breaking down into disordered bands again. Groups of four were coming for me now instead of a single group. None of this was good news, I knew they worked well together in groups like that, and if any of them caught me I would be detained long enough for the rest to join in the battle. Four to one, I liked my odds, but five groups of four to one was suicide. I didn't have one big slow Scion but twenty agile and ferocious ones.

My only chance was to get away and live to fight again. I tried to throw a few fireballs behind me as I ran but they were too quick. I couldn't catch any of them off guard. I could see the clearing to my trailer. I could also feel them getting close enough the hairs on the back of my neck stood up. I threw two more timed fireballs to slow them down but each group seemed to get out the way like they knew it was coming. I was out of juice, I don't think I had enough power left in me to throw a matchbook at them let alone a fireball. I ran anyway. I wasn't going to give up just because my power was fading. I could run and cover ground quick with just a few steps. I felt one coming down from the tree and smacked it aside in midair with my staff. I still had my training and physical power left but my legs had started a whole body shiver. My legs were starting to buckle now that all sensation left them. It wasn't painful anymore which meant I could be facing frostbite at the least. The running helped a little, but my muscles were getting colder instead of warming up. I knew it was over. I was going to have to stand against all twenty. It was suicide but it was my suicide. I wouldn't be remembered as the one that died running away.

I was about to claim my stomping ground then I felt something I had never felt before. I tried to see the wall of energy that was directly behind me, but it was like an invisible sword sliced through the air. I could see trees split in half by the wall. I scanned around, I wasn't alone again, only this wasn't the slithery feeling I got when I felt the Scions. It was more of a feather on the cheek, something soft and amazing, but it was reinforced with steel. I tried to find the source with no luck. The Scions didn't hit it like a wall and slide down, they just slowed down to a comical freeze frame. I took half a second to register what I had seen, but I decided getting out of there was better. It didn't hurt that I heard a strong bass-filled voice just repeating the word "Go." in my head. I didn't want to waste time and ran straight into the trailer and began snatching what I could carry. The temporary warmth of the trailer made my legs scream. I kept everything packed in my suitcase, but I didn't have time to search for anything else I might have left lying around. I had been living straight out of the suitcase after my California adventure. I could feel the first Scion pop loose of the wall and more were just behind him. I grabbed the car keys and settled my frozen legs in the seat and floorboard. I could barely tell they were there. "Hope you're up to driving a stick." I said to my legs, obviously because they were their own entity. I looked to my side just in time to see my neighbor one last time. Would he get out OK?

I tried to reason this out but then I noticed he didn't look greasy anymore. The hat was gone and his clothes were solid white. He held out a hand with sweat rolling down his forehead. On his hip wasn't the claw hammer he wore to work but a freaking sword. An ornate antique sword with a scabbard and all. I pulled the car door closed and spun from the parking lot. I got to the highway heading back west hoping to lose them by doubling back. I looked up just in time to see a sign that said forty west. Guess I was heading back to the mid-west. At least it would be warmer there. I wondered absently if I had one of those energy string things attached to me. Would I know?

CHAPTER TWENTY-THREE

I drove like my life depended on it, it probably did. I stopped for gas, restroom, and quick foods and drinks. I didn't dare stay anywhere for long, everywhere I went there were people who could get hurt if I was caught. I couldn't risk another Huntsville, killing these demons was one thing but innocent people getting hurt was something totally different. I drove until I saw a sign for Las Vegas. I am still not sure what made me go that way, it would be even worse with the number of people there. I just knew that was my next stop. I was delirious with pain in my legs, exhaustion, sleep deprivation, and fear. I was worse than a drunk behind the wheel when I got to Vegas. Everything was hazy, and double vision had forced me to drive with one hand over my eye. I nearly hit two people with such a limited range of sight. I turned onto a side street of gorgeous houses. This had to have been some kind of high roller area or something. I had never seen houses like these before. High gated and high walled yards to protect privacy. My vision must have been going out entirely when I stopped. The house in front of me had a halo effect surrounding it. I couldn't drive any further, but I also knew that I couldn't stay in my car. I had a big enough target on my back, staying with the car would just add to it, and being unconscious in my car I didn't want to think about how that would turn out. I grabbed my staff and the Bible and scaled the wall. I remember hitting the ground; I vaguely remember clutching the Bible and the staff close so I wouldn't drop them. Then everything went black.

I woke up in a bed, the tips of my hair were damp and I could smell chlorine. I looked up and for a minute thought I was seeing the Hollywood version of an Angel. A beautiful face framed by flowing red hair, thick lips spread in a 'too pretty to be real' smile. I could tell she wasn't tall, at least by my distorted version of height. She seemed to just be waiting for my voice to start working. She still had a roll of gauze in her hand and the handsome man with the short cut hair who was helping her, had medical scissors. Did I luck out and find a doctor. I could feel something on the backs of my legs but the fronts of my legs were still numb, tingly feeling. I looked down and saw that both legs were generously covered by gauze and the faint smell of antibiotic cream. "I'm glad to see you doin better, sweetie." She had an amazingly cheerful voice full of a Canadian accent and sweetness. I had the unconscious urge to hear her say about, I knew it would sound so perfectly Canadian with her bubbly voice. "My names Lechelle, what's yours sweetie?" she asked. I could hear the sounds of others rustling behind her in the other room and the sound of pool balls clacking. "Cheryl" I choked out barely able to even say that much.

She handed me a clear soda. How perfect, I thought to myself. After a few careful sips of the bubbly drink I managed to get my voice back enough to ask her "How did I get here?" She laughed, even her laugh was friendly. "I was going ta ask you the same thing. You're a long way from anywhere you could have got frostbite that bad. The license plates on your car say Tennessee, but you surely didn't drive all this way with those wounds. She gestured at my arm and legs. I hadn't even realized I had hurt my arm let alone that badly. She had everything dressed and patched the best any hospital would have done. "How did you know how to help me?" I asked lamely. "We're from Canada; frostbite is a little more normal for us up there. I thought for sure my accent would give it away." she replied still keeping her voice soft. Before I could ask, She pointed to the bedside. My Bible and staff were both there as well as what was left of my clothes. I was dressed in shorts and a man's t-shirt. The shirt was pretty close to my size. I noticed it said "I'm here, what were your other two wishes?" I laughed weakly. "It's music to hear you laugh. Do you need anything? Food, more pop, anyone we can call?" I said "No" more forcefully than I meant to. She didn't even blink, "OK sweetie, I will let you get some rest. We aren't going anywhere until you are better. Just say my name, and I will do what I can to get here quickly.

I fell back to sleep even though I really wanted to get somewhere alone in case the demons showed up again. When I would wake up I scanned for them a few times and couldn't feel anything around. There were bad vibes but they were a long way off, probably on the strip. It is Sin City after all. I could also for the first time feel good vibes. They were close but I couldn't put my finger on where exactly.

I stayed in bed for two days. I could feel my energy coming back. I also kept thinking about the odds of me climbing a random wall in the middle of Las Vegas, land in the yard of a friendly Canadian family who recognized frostbite, and knew how to treat it better than the local hospital. I remembered the urging to head this way, the halo around the house. It was like I was meant to run out of energy and strength right then. I filed that away for my list of questions if I ever got to talk to Father Ryan again. Then something clicked in my head. Father Ryan.

That was the name of a school in Nashville. I read something about him once for a field trip mom didn't let me go on when I was a kid. Again with the random, He was a preacher during the Civil War, on the wrong side. Not sure what it meant but I was certain somehow that it mattered. I tried to find something in the Bible to help. It had done me well so far. I dug through it but couldn't find a reference to the Amon that the

MegaScion mentioned. I wondered if that is what was meant by stopping the liar. Maybe they were both in there, but I couldn't find it.

I was beginning to get the feeling that I had been fighting Amon's demons, But Belial had engineered it. That way if I was eliminated, Belial could take the credit for the chess move, and if I won he could show the weakness of Amon's troops as a means of usurping his throne. That was the only thing that made sense for the two very different type of Scion attacks. The next problem to figure out was how the demons were tracking me. I know, thanks to Juan the demon, that they were using the Rod of Moses to track me, but how had they tracked me to Tennessee? They could have honed in on my new fighting staff but I doubted it. They didn't know I made it, so they wouldn't have been looking for something that didn't exist. I had only spoken to Juan the Demon boy, but that didn't track. He wasn't interested in this fight. He saw it as an outsider; I doubt he would have bothered to help either side out. He wouldn't have told me so much if he was interested in my destruction. I couldn't think of what else I had done that would have alerted them to my position. Not knowing this stuff sucks bad.

Lechelle was the best, she made sure I had food, didn't push me for information, and was content to see me doing well. I guessed her age to be maybe thirty, She had the curves of a fifties pinup model, I wish I had those, I was far too tall and malnourished to have curves that looked that good without some really good medical enhancements. I spent so much time running now, even in practice, to have any curves again. I never saw her without a smile on her face. On the third day she came in and told me that they would be going back home soon. I had learned that her whole family had come here with her for vacation though only the cute girl with pink hair looked young enough to be her child. Maybe the rest were cousins or something. I didn't want to presume to ask too much. She had already done so much to help me but let me keep my privacy. "I need to get back on the road soon, there are some people I have to protect and I can't do it if I am here." I said. I wasn't lying, I just left off the part that her family were the people, and getting away from them was protection enough. I could see a slight frown but she instantly perked back up. "Well then, maybe we can help get you on your way." She yelled for the men to come help me get my stuff back to my car.

My car was inside the gate hiding it from street view. All of the family were too good to be true. They all wore smiles, all looked like they should have been models. The men had that eternal youth thing going for them like Lechelle; I couldn't even begin to guess what relation they were. I used my staff like a walking stick to help me to the car. I was doing better but still felt weak. I looked into my car, she was spotless. Detailed was a better word for it. She looked almost new inside and out and had a beautiful new blingy gearshift knob. I hugged them all and stopped for an extra second to thank Lechelle again. She smiled and acted like she hadn't done anything out of the ordinary. She clearly didn't know how rare nice people really were.

I got in the car wanting to put some distance between myself and this wonderful family. If they were caught up in my chaos infested life, I would never be able to forgive myself. I think I met my first evidence of real Angels here on earth. Not the sword wielding neighbors, or dream talking kind. The ones that don't know that they are. I pulled out of the gate and the biggest man closed the gate behind me. I swore I could see Lechelle's eyes in my rear view longer than they should have been there. I still felt the good vibe feeling around me, like I had some kind of guard circling my car at seventy miles an hour as I left Las Vegas and headed west.

CHAPTER TWENTY-FOUR

I drove until I saw the California state line. I went completely on impulse. When I thought about where I was going for a second, I made a conscious decision to put myself as far away from innocent bystanders as I could. I didn't want to put anyone in the line of fire, except myself. I saw a sign that inspired me, it wasn't all glowey or otherwise magical except in my own head. "Sequoia National Park 100 miles" was a good enough sign for me. I had plenty of food to make it there a while, and there would be cabins this time of year not being used. I originally had an urge to hit Death Valley, it was on my bucket list, but I couldn't make myself go to a possible fight to the death in a place called 'Death' anything. That would make me look as ridiculous as the Scions.

I found what I was looking for, an old disused cabin. I took my trunk full of groceries I picked up before getting to the reserve. I felt out and couldn't sense anything evil for as far as I could tell. I knew it wasn't foolproof, but I knew it worked for the ones trying to shred my favorite clothes as well as my body. I got myself settled in as comfortable as living off the grid can be. There was no bed and only an old hand pump out back for water. It was rusted, but I managed to break the pump free after some creative coaxing from a tire iron. I had planned for the lack of a bed. Sleeping on anything ground based would have just been an invitation to critters. I couldn't stand the thought of them crawling around on me as I slept. I know my hammock wasn't a perfect solution, but it was comfy. Next I put out the industrial sized pack of wet wipes, and got the place in some sort of livable condition.

I made trips once a week back to civilization. It was obvious everything was a tourist trap around here, but I really didn't want to drive too far away into city centers. I also made it a point to get as much web information as I could about Amon and Belial, as well as the ArchAngels, while I was in town to read later. I didn't want to freak the country people out by asking about Demons and Angels. That would be a sure way to get a lot of attention I didn't need.

I did find a church though. It didn't have the creepy feeling some of the others had. Some people dressed in jeans some in more traditional church attire. One young woman was the greeting party. standing by the doorway, I couldn't help but imagine an excitable puppy waiting for you to open the door. She was thin like a long distance runner, high cheekbones, black hair, and a soft caramel coloring that was nearly matched by the color of her eyes. Her blue skirt and pink ruffled top clashed splendidly. It put me at ease but also drove home how much I changed since my birthday. I would have never left the house wearing pants with an unintentional tear in them.

Was I really losing my mind?

She walked up to me like we were old friends, and began pointing people out to me. Her voice wasn't what you would call melodious, it was deeper, scratchier. She probably used to smoke fairly heavily, though I couldn't smell even a hint of stale tobacco on her. In one hand she held a Bible, much newer and smaller than my own. It had oversized letters on the cover like mine though. The hand she used to point everyone out was holding a small plastic chip. I guess the reservations weren't too far from here. I wondered vaguely how valuable a bronze chip was. Gambling was another big taboo growing up with mom.

I watched as her skirt swished back and forth every time she twisted to point in another direction. There was more patch work on her skirt than original fabric. It took nearly a minute before I was able to ask her name. She seemed more concerned that I knew everyone else. I didn't have much experience with people being friendly quite to this level. "You can just call me Maureen." she said with a smile. When she smiled it wasn't a happy smile, maybe more of a comfortable smile. She knew who and what she was, and that was OK with her. She looked down at my Bible and made an oooh expression with her lips without any noise. I held it up for her to see better. I wasn't going to get taken in by anything that couldn't touch the Bible. The ones that couldn't touch it, never had answers for me that weren't new riddles. She took it into her hands and ran her fingers over the leather and then began lightly turning pages.

I confess I was slow on the uptake. She could barely see the Bible in front of her. Something about her eyes never focused quite right. When she looked back up at me I wondered what she saw. She seemed fine pointing out the Johnson family in their perfectly pressed shirts and flowery dresses, the Rosemill's and their denim shirts and faded blue jean pants. I finally took in the entirety of the church and counted thirteen sets of pews. She probably knew without looking where everyone would be. People tend to be creatures of habit as well.

Maureen looked at me the same way the priest that healed me at the first soup kitchen I visited. She could make out my general shape but from her height I must have looked like a column. "Your Bible is the oldest I have held, is it in English?" I never thought about the Bible being written in different languages. "Yes, I can't read any other languages, it's an heirloom." I waited for a lightning bolt to strike. It didn't need to. "Just not from your family." she said in a little quieter voice. There was no question. Somehow, she knew it hadn't been in my possession long. She was the fourth person I met so far that just knew stuff. She was the first that wasn't a priest, Angel, or demon boy though. "Where did you find such an amazing copy of the good book?" I tried to come up with a lie; my mouth just ran ahead of my brain. "Father Ryan in Florida gave it to me." "And I bet your life hasn't been the same since then has it?" she asked. She didn't know how right she was. The way she looked around my outline seemed to suggest otherwise. "No it hasn't"

CHAPTER TWENTY-FIVE

I looked forward to the talks with Maureen each week. The local preacher wasn't bad either. He seemed nice and didn't act pushy at all. He just seemed grateful for another pair of ears to hear his sermon. The one thing that didn't escape my attention, Maureen's smile changed when he walked behind the podium. He wasn't a striking figure. Shorter than many women I knew, balding and blue eye's that verged more to the gray end of the color spectrum. Judging from Maureen's smile, I would say she had a bit of a crush. Neither of them wore wedding bands either. The sermon was good, and it covered a little of what I already knew. He talked about Moses leading his people into the desert for forty years but giving up hope and faith that they would ever get there. Maureen knew every verse by heart. She told me more about Moses when I asked about his staff, other miracles It was known to perform. She didn't seem to like the notion of a magic staff as much. I backpedaled as quick as I could with a promise to return next Sunday.

Some of the guys in the stories she told me were serious butt kickers. She told me the story of Samson and several others that had their faith tested. I couldn't help shivering a little when I heard what happened to Lot's wife. The overall tone was forgiveness. That put me more at ease. The part that didn't put me at ease was the lack of any real stories of women doing something amazing. I couldn't shake the feeling some of the names had been changed to protect the poor defenseless women. Knowing my mom, that was probably why she never let me go to church as a kid even when my friends invited me. Mom was all about women being able to do anything a man could do. Being raised by her and seeing her do the maintenance they showed on TV as "man's work" I think I knew why. I never really thought about mom not dating. She talked about dad like he was still around, just unavailable.

The story of Abraham almost sacrificing his son made me cringe hard enough to find a reason to leave. The story of Cain was one of the more interesting ones. Sibling rivalry was something I heard about but being an only child I guess I couldn't quite understand it. I always thought if I had a sister, she would be my best friend. Maureen talked about the brothers fighting. How Cain slew Abel over his choice in a wife, and then lied to God about it. That was the end of the similarities with what I read though. She insisted that Cain killed Abel with a rock instead of a plow blade. I asked if that was like the fight between Loki and Thor. She rubbed her thick eyebrows pushing back the headache I am sure my ignorance created. That was something she did every time I asked a stupid question. "Those are Norse myths created by the Vikings before they learned about God." She didn't say it forcefully, but there was a finality to her words. It was time to listen and learn, not ask stupid questions.

Every time I thought I was getting the hang of Christianity, my ignorance would pop up with a wonderful question about how Buddha fit in the Bible. A few of my better ones actually made her laugh. I did love hearing her laugh. There was a bit of a dull sermon the third Sunday I was there and I asked Maureen why she didn't preach. She seemed to know everything about it and her stories could hold you in place until she was done. That drew the biggest laugh from her. I noticed she did something odd though; she shifted nervously in the pew before she answered. Until that point she seemed forever comfortable in her spot on the pew. Now it was like a hot seat. Did I say something bad? It was probably bound to happen. "Women rarely become priests; the closest most get is marrying a priest. Besides I think Pastor Bentley is just about perfect" So she did have the hots for him. I wondered why she didn't just say something. Then I thought about her eyesight. She probably didn't feel worthy. "Oh, I thought preachers couldn't marry. I am so confused." I said. "That's the Catholics sweetie." "Oh, what's the difference?" "About two hours." she said leaving me more confused and then laughed at her own joke. I was even more sure Maureen was biding her time until the preacher noticed he couldn't get by without her. I would never wait for a man to ask me, if I wanted to marry him. Of course if there was anything I knew less about than religion, it was men.

After that day I decided not to embarrass myself with trying to understand the factions, and variations on religion. I stuck to what I already knew. If a giant Kali jumped up to kill me I'd worry about it then. I wasn't sure what a Kali was, but the name stuck in my head. That worried me, names I never read or heard of popped into my head sometimes. Sanity, don't leave me just yet, if you are still there at all.

I didn't go back after that. Though I did see a notice on the church sign congratulating the preacher on getting engaged one day while getting supplies. I'm not sure why, but I felt like I learned all I was going to need for now. There was nothing on my radar involving Samson, or the hundreds of other stories I learned from Maureen. Maybe it wasn't the stories I was supposed to be learning but the feeling from the people there. I felt a little guilty when I passed Maureen coming out of a liquor store a few weeks later with shorter man in a black outfit on her arm. Maybe she finally caught her preacher. I knew she couldn't see me but there wasn't exactly a million little sports cars running around this area

CHAPTER TWENTY-SIX

I did OK for a few months living like this, I learned how to fix broken strands on my hammock. I kept up my running and exercise; it managed to keep me alive so far. I don't know if I have ever been so relaxed. I even made the cabin livable. I became so comfortable, I seriously debated getting curtains. There was so much area around me and I could reach out and feel the demons well before they got close. Covering my line of sight through the numerous windows seemed like a bad idea. I didn't find much else out about the demons in my research but I was sure who saved my rear in Tennessee. The sword and his general demeanor, it had to have been Michael. He was the serious butt-kicker up that way. I learned the lesson from my dream heaven trip and didn't say any of the names out loud. It seemed to give them some measure of power or got their attention or something to that effect. Even though I was sure the ArchAngels were on my side, no attention was better than the wrong attention. Maureen taught me that not all of the ArchAngels stayed good and one even managed to be thrown out of the house, so to speak.

I liked the solitude after all this time of running from one fight to another. Not embarrassing myself was another plus. It was nearly ten months since I saw my first Scion. It felt like the entirety of my life. My old life never truly existed, except for a prelude to this. Who knows, maybe all of this is still a hallucination of some kind or mental madness and I am really in the county psychiatric ward. I bet I would make a great patient. Everyone I met was a Demon, Angel, or something in between, instead of doctor, nurse, and other patients. Father Ryan was probably my psychiatrist in disguise.

Even in the sticks it was bound to happen. "Umm hello?" came a young voice from outside the cabin. I poked my head out and put on my best smile. "Hi, I'm not used to company when I visit out here." I lied. I decided that she couldn't know how long I stayed here. People dropped off the map all the time though. I reasoned in my head that if she thought I just got here and was on vacation from a real job maybe she would go away happy. When I spun my head the to the voices direction, I saw what I really didn't want to see. A ranger uniform. A tall black woman with the stunning looks of a runway model looked back at me. She even had a notebook out. "I don't see this campsite as being used." double crap, a well-informed ranger. "Hang on let me get dressed." I lied again. It was getting too easy to lie. I searched everywhere. I found the paperwork from my weekly admittance into the area, That was going to have to do. The car what about the car, it would have been seen coming in and leaving every week. I knew someone was watching out for me and helped with paperwork. Finding both a car rental agreement and an updated cabin rental agreement was stretching it. Someone wasn't just watching out for me, they were making sure the mortal authorities stayed out of the way entirely.

I came out and put on my best smile. I was trying to be careful not to look like I was getting away with something. I stopped halfway in between and went for flustered. That was real enough. I wouldn't have to fake that. "Hi Ms." I read her badge. "Danara" "Actually that is Ranger Danara out here." Great I got the hard ass that had to prove herself even when she was alone. I went for flustered and sheepish. "Here are my rental papers for the car and the cabin." I said while looking down. I couldn't win today. I could see why she was so bitter the moment I looked down. There was a patch of white scarred skin flowing up her leg and it peeked out of the short sleeve of her Ranger shirt. She looked like she was burned horribly before.

Working out here probably meant a careless camper and their bonfire caused it, which might explain the attitude. She scoffed at my paperwork, though I am sure it was the genuine article. She would have had a problem with anything at this point. I was prepared for her tirade and posturing. It just never came. She looked over her notepad, then the paperwork I handed her. She brightened into a smile that didn't fit with her previous mood. "I have him now, that smug bastard Brad will get what is coming to him." She handed the paperwork back to me and walked a circle inside the cabin. I saw my paperwork was signed by a Brad Scribble. The last name flowed into a curvy line instead of actual letters. "I will get him fired for this one. Not entering a camper on the log is a top offense. Mr. Perfect did it now." she nearly yelled as she came out. I am sure the cougars and bears really cared. I had to stifle a laugh when some part of my brain wanted to ask her if she had a picnic basket stealing bear to harass instead. I managed to keep that to myself. I wanted to defend this poor kid, and then I thought about having to put up with "Ranger Danara" every day. I was probably doing him a favor. It wasn't as if this part of the country was lacking in parks that needed rangers. She got in her Eco-friendly electric car, and only the sound of the rocks under her tires made any noise. That was how she snuck up on me.

She was barely over the hill when I went back inside the cabin thinking I needed to work harder and go on the offensive, instead of hiding like prey. She snuck up on me pretty easily. Had I really let myself get too comfortable? I needed to hunt the Scions down. I was just prolonging the inevitable. I didn't realize until the roof caved in above me in a burst of red flames, that my scare was too little, too late. First I wondered if she got away clean or did the Scions kill her just to make the way clear. I didn't have time to wonder about that any further as the old place went into full flame like those movies they show you around Christmas about the dangers of indoor trees and hot lights. I grabbed my staff and ran out of the cabin. I was hit square in the chest and sent flying to the right side by a wrecking ball. I noticed his white blonde hair and his gaunt but muscular sinew. The hair just seemed wrong on a creature that really didn't have skin. Belial's Scions again. At least they were more flammable than the spiked ones.

I reached out for the first time in months. I became so used to being alone, I wasn't even doing basic scans anymore. There were five here, the fifth was really strong but just standing well away from the battle like a general. I knew it had to be Amon or Belial. A full demon was the only thing that could feel that strong. The one that sucker punched me was strong, but when we hit the ground I tucked into a roll. I popped back up with enough energy to obliterate him. I aimed and tried to hit him with a burst of flame, but he deftly jumped out of the way, like he knew it was coming. That was when I sensed the small lines of power. It traveled from him and the others I couldn't see back to the big demon. I was about to do the same move that helped me with the MegaScion, cutting the cord that tied it to the parent demon fueling it. Then I had a flash of inspiration. The tendrils of power gave me something I wasn't used to having. True knowledge of exactly where they were at all times. The second thing it gave me was an order to the fight. When I cut the MegaScion off from its controller, the twenty Scions that made up the MegaScion seemed to go mad and attacked in ways that only individual predators all chasing the same prey might. The Scions may be more cunning with a demon controlling their actions but now they were tagged and organized too. I changed tactics to a dodge and burn method. I dodged the attacker when I felt it coming but instead of attacking back, I hit one of the others positioning for their chance to attack.

The greater demon didn't seem to catch what I was doing so far. He must have thought it a lucky shot or the fool had let me see him. So far so good, I ducked another attack but the female tucked and changed direction behind me, she rolled then sprang up behind me while the remaining male went high. I felt my thighs rip in four high arcs. The nerves that should have never recovered were back to full working order. Yay me. Any lower and she would have got a tendon and that would have been the end of it. Not much of a consolation as my legs screamed in pain. I tried to jump as the next female came in, but found jumping wasn't an option anymore. I was forced to fall very ungracefully to my right and roll instead. I used the staff to help me spring back up and pushed a small amount of wind through the staff instead of staying on the ground. Another strike came where I had been standing and I swung both arms down at the same time hitting him with the biggest fireball I could create.

I heard crackling behind me. My cabin was in full flame with everything inside. I could hear the pop of the canned food exploding in the heat. Crap, all my stuff was in there. It distracted me, which was probably the secondary reason for setting the roof on fire, the first was to make me run into this ambush. I spun out of the way as one of the females whizzed by so fast I barely recognized which one she was. The other was already on her way back in. They attacked like wild dogs in a pack. That meant the one who had just missed me was turning for her next attack as the one attacking kept my attention. I spun and followed the now thicker tendril of energy toward the one turning for an attack and hit her with a blast of wind mid stride, followed by another fireball. She wasn't going to dodge this one. I put a little too much into it. I blasted her into the air and what was left fell into powder. I could feel the band strengthen between the remaining one and the greater demon. She turned her head to look at the remains of her partner and I threw my staff like a javelin straight into her chest. Flames covering the entire length of it. She screamed, it sounded nothing like a human scream. It echoed through the ground like an earthquake. I felt the band of power snap like a rubber band as she burst into flames and turned to a smattering of ash. I ran to get my staff with my legs in blinding pain and couldn't sense the greater demon anymore.

CHAPTER TWENTY-SEVEN

It took a moment, but I finally decided on a course of action. Thankfully I left the keys in the car; it wasn't like someone was going to sneak up on me in the middle of a freaking forest. Oh yeah, so basically it was that kind of thinking that got me in this mess. I decided I was done running and need to figure out how to hit them like they hit me, I just wasn't sure how to do that, but you know, details. The one thing I knew for sure was I wasn't getting anywhere running, from place to place, hiding until they somehow found me again. Going back down to Hell wasn't an option. I don't think I would survive long in the unfamiliar territory. I like having home field advantage. I know asking the ArchAngels for help was as useful as talking to myself, they couldn't do anything but follow orders. I didn't want to embarrass myself further with Maureen. Even mentioning a Demon or ArchAngel speaking to a human seemed to be some kind of heresy.

I almost thought about Juan again and then remembered the fire in his eyes at our last encounter and doubted he would greet me in much of a great mood if I looked for him. I definitely wasn't going back to Huntsville. The pregnant pauses in Father Richardson's speech were enough to make a ten minute answer take hours. I was down to one person/spirit/whatever and I trusted him less and less lately. I am not sure why, when we first met, I was sure he was one of the good guys. After talking with Maureen though, I wasn't as sure. I am sure there had been plenty of Father Ryan's in the past and he wasn't necessarily the one I remembered from some long ago history class. What was the old saying though, any port in the storm? I thought of his balding head, his warm smile, his reassuring demeanor, and I nearly wrecked my car going eighty when he just showed up in the passenger seat, seat belt and all. He acted as though he was sitting there the whole time and I just turned to realize it.

"Good Evening Angel." he said calmly. "Father Ryan, where did ... never mind, hello to you too." I should have been used to this by now. I had seen both Angel and demons make entrances like this too regularly over the last year. It still didn't make it easier. I tried to act all nonchalant about it but the car skidding back into the correct lane kind of gave the air of normalcy away. "And what dire thing are we running from today?" He asked in the closest thing to a gruff manner I had heard yet from him. "I got jumped by four puppet Scions in Sequoia. I think I'm tired of running and I'm looking for a way to be the hunter this time instead of the prey. Any ideas come to mind?" I nearly snarled the last part unintentionally. I really didn't mean any ill will towards the priest. I think I was just too tired to care. He sat with his fingers steepled, which I knew meant that he was thinking. I am pretty sure we sat like this for five miles in dead silence, which in his case would just be silence, right? "I think you have already made your choice Angel, instead of hunting down the puppet master you have chosen to run from him once again. If you really want to hunt him down you have to get his name and battle him yourself. You do know, that you have been quite the conversation piece on both sides." he said without releasing the steepled pose with his hands. I couldn't think without moving my hands, let alone hold entire conversations.

"I think I know who is behind it." I said. "Who would that be child?" he asked with more animation than I had seen in him yet. I almost said the name, and then I remembered what the dream Angel guy had said. "I can't say the name out loud right here. It gives them power, it might even bring them to me, I am still a little fuzzy on that." I said, proud of my knowledge of this stuff. "Very good Angel, you are learning. Do you feel that you have the power to take on any who would have the strength to bind such Scions to themselves? You haven't got enough power to bind anyone to your side yet. Logically, that would mean they are a much greater power than you and would probably swat you like a fly. I would hate to see that happen again." he said the last with some somberness, as if he were truly sorry for something that had already occurred. "So your saying to stay the course, and play whack-a-mole?" I asked not thinking that he may not understand the reference. "If you mean running to fight another day until they run out of foot soldiers, yes, that is precisely what I am saying. Until you come up with a better idea, that is."

We sat in the car a little longer, I thought about what he said and he sat there patient as a, well, priest. I thought about his reference to binding someone to my aid. I can't say it was a bad idea to get some help. It was the binding part I didn't like. "What do you mean binding, isn't that the thing demons do, not Angels, Sprites, or whatever I am?" I asked. "Even humans do it just not so overtly, do CEO's have a flock of people ready to do whatever they are told, do priests have a flock of people that are hanging on their every word, or do presidents have a flock of people ready to jump in front of a bullet for them? You see Angel, there is little difference in these. The flock has free will to do what they want, it is up to their shepherd to guide them in the right directions to best aid themselves. It really is selfless and beneficial for both sides." he finished with a bit of a grin. I could see all of these as being reasonable, and he wasn't wrong. The Demons just did it more forcefully. They bound wills, where the humans bound hearts. I guess in Hell there wasn't an abundance of heart to bind.

"Do you mind if I ask one more question?" I

asked trying to remain polite. "Of course." he replied gently. "Why did the Scions in Florida mention killing all but the last of my kind? From what I have gathered there haven't been any others like me before." I asked. Again with the steepled hands and silence. I knew it wasn't a slight or meant to be taken badly, but I felt like we were racing against time and didn't need to take pregnant pauses between each answer. He sat looking out the passenger window so I couldn't see his expressions but I heard his voice. "The Scions have no concept of time, you are familiar with the Seraphim and the great cleansing?" he asked. "You mean the great flood? Yeah, I have read the stories." "Well then you know there were many battles back then between Scions and Seraphim, The battles became so great the entire towns were destroyed along with everyone in them. Once the Seraphim were gone from the face of the earth the Scions had little reason to leave Hell.

The Scions don't see you any different. Only as an expression of an Angel who walks the earth instead of above it. Names do not mean much to the ones of many names. Only their true name matters so they let themselves be called Scions, they let themselves be called Amon. They still get power from such propped up names, but only their true name is of any real power." he finished. I was shocked he used Amon's name so casually. I thought about what Juan the Demon boy had said about positioning and strategy in the underworld. It was like he was pointing me at the real enemy, Amon, but hadn't Juan shown me that Amon had many thrones beneath his own. Could I trust a Demon boy over a ghostly priest who had never done anything but help me when I needed it. "If you intend on facing him down, you will need to turn the car around and go back to get his trail. I must go now, I have much to do. Time is not quite as binding for me now, but it is still the bit I pull against." he said. With that he was gone. No goodbye, just gone. I needed to think but I also needed some radio to cloud out the distracting thoughts. I pulled in for gas at a small station, read the "sorry, we don't accept credit cards right now." sign in all block letters. As if I still had a credit card to use.

I filled up and started heading back the way I came, and then I heard one of those screechy emergency noises from the radio. Right in the middle of one of my favorite songs too. "Attention." the overly masculine voice announced. "The forest fire at Sequoia has been extinguished. Arson is suspected. If you see a woman with red hair approximately six foot tall. Please call the local authorities as she is wanted for questioning. She was last seen in a Fiat 500." First I was in shock. That was the third purpose of the fire. In case I did escape, plenty of people had seen me going in and out of the area. Though Maureen couldn't see well, everyone else at that church knew what I looked like. I don't think they would be so hospitable to the woman that threatened their town with fire.

Then I was indignant, I didn't drive one of those little Italian death boxes. My Mini was the real thing. She was way better than those silly little cheap knock offs. To add to it, I was six foot one, thank you very much. I haven't been six foot since sophomore year in high school. They got the hair color right but I could change it enough to avoid suspicion. I stopped on the side of the road to turn around. That was when I realized what had bothered me from the conversation with the Father. Binding something to your will. He had made valid reasoning's for each except they all involved people using their free will to choose. The Scions didn't have free will. Binding was pretty much the opposite. I bet the Scions couldn't just quit and go work for the other guys if they wanted to. So now I was stuck. My only source for actual help might not be who he seems, I am a wanted woman now, and have to do exactly what the demons want me to, whether I like it or not. Just call me a coward. I ran like a rabbit.

CHAPTER TWENTY-EIGHT

Who was worse, the lesser evil as it were. Amon was obviously very powerful, he would not have gotten where he was otherwise. I still didn't know much about him. Something I ran into early trying to dig up information was the lack of agreement about Hell and its constituent players. I guess if disinformation was good enough for the governments to use, Hell probably invented it. I thought about all of the information I had, it was too much to tackle altogether. So it became a math problem, I loved math and it was how I thought anyway. I know X and Y but need Z. This wasn't something I should try to work out on the road. First I had to find a place to stop. Weatherford, Texas it was. Far enough from the hectic pace of Dallas and Fort Worth, but still close enough for the amenities I needed.

I packed all my stuff into the shabby little hotel room. This one might be worse than the one in Tennessee. I was afraid to sit on the bed, I was sure it was infested with all manners of creepy crawlers. I thought about each piece that I had so far. I knew that Juan didn't seem interested in the outcome and actually did something to help me. I knew that Belial was much lower than Amon and was also called the prince of lies. I knew the Scions had been a different type. The ones with white hair fought very differently to the ones with spikes. The sinewed ones were much more feral, more animal like. The ones that turned into the MegaScion and the teleporting ones were more cunning and planned further ahead. I tried to get a signal on my phone while I was waiting for the hair dye to set. No use, no matter how high I held it in the air, or how I stood on one foot contorting for one lonely bar. Hmm, a bar sounded nice. Had it been a full year since my first experience with the Scions. I looked at the date on my phone, how had I forgotten my own birthday.

I rinsed out my hair and it came out more multi-toned, than the flat brown look on the box. Oh well, it's just hair. I definitely didn't look like myself anymore. I could walk in a police station with a sketch taped to my shirt and not be identified now. They say brunette's can be fun and exciting. I hadn't felt much like fun, but it was my birthday. I felt out for any presence. Nothing evil, and I was getting good range on it here. I could feel good and bad parts of people now, not just demons. I looked at myself in the mirror. The clothes were a little baggy, but it was Texas, so I tied a knot in the back of my shirt to fit my waist better. I wasn't buying my own birthday drink tonight. I needed the down time, the human time.

I walked into some bar with half a sign on its roof. It could have been the Dew Drop Inn for all I cared. I went in and handed security my ID. "Nice try mouse, but this ain't you." he said with his overly masculine bouncer voice. "Yes it is." I said defensively. "Have you never heard of hair color before?" He seemed to take this in; scratching at the laminate like it would come off. "C'mon, it's my Birthday. Can't a girl get a drink on her birthday?" I said in my sweetest voice. He took one more look at the date and stamped my hand handing me back the ID. "Be straight or you're the first to go mouse. We don't need underage trouble here." he said. I just gave him my best smile and walked straight to the bar. What part of me resembled a mouse? I was tall, now brown haired adjacent, and strong. I had a mouse when I was a kid. It was gray, short, and liked to jump a lot.

I looked around, the people were younger than I expected. I am not sure what I expected, sawdust on the floor, peanut shells, country music, and clientele old enough to be my grandparents. Instead the walls were covered by psychedelic posters in black-light, a large dance floor, and dance music. There were women here with every shade of hair you could imagine. I must be near a college judging from the average age of the bar.

The bar was packed with people shouting drink orders. This was probably going to be a short visit. I only brought a twenty with me and this place was half women. Oh well, happy birthday gin and tonic for me. I ordered my drink and braced for a college bar price. The bartender returned with my drink, smiling. He didn't say anything and just dropped a napkin in front of the drink instead of under it and a note scrawled in precise lettering that could have come from a computer. It just said "End of bar, man with white hat and blue shirt." A free drink was good, I wasn't planning on getting drunk, but if I came out of here with my birthday drink and a story I would be happy.

That would be my luck anyway, to be attacked by Scions while on all fours, swearing to never drink again. I walked down to thank the man for the drink. He was tall, as tall as I was. Nice butt too, I tapped him on the shoulder and Juan turned around smiling. "Happy Birthday, Cheryl." I nearly dropped my drink, then I almost threw it in his face for the last meeting. It would be a waste of good alcohol though. I settled on a scowl.

He motioned to a table, and pulled out a chair for me. He pulled the next closest one out and sat in it himself. Most men sit across from you, I don't know why, it is harder to actually have a conversation that way. "I know you are full of questions Cheryl, but tonight just enjoy a small reprieve and a bit of normalcy." he said calmly. I couldn't argue that I needed it, or the company. "Yeah, it is perfectly normal to get hit on by a demon boy in a bar." I said with only a tiny bit of sarcasm in my voice, I swear. He laughed, oh dear lord that laugh. It was intoxicating, it was like watching a puppy do something cute and not say aw. I smiled for the first time in forever at his laughter.

"Only one rule tonight, you are safe, but no shop talk. You are just Cheryl, I am just Juan." he said resting his hands on the table around his own drink. "You do know that eliminates every piece of small talk I know right, what do you do? Uh huh that sounds amazing. What are your hobbies? Oh, I have always been fascinated by that." I finished with a strong drink from my glass.

He laughed again before replying. "Actually I am a mediator of sorts, I am also interested in stamps and coins. I like cats and wish I could have one. So you see Cheryl, there is still small talk to be had." I gulped a little; it was easier when he was just a demon errand boy. That may have been the point of all this to begin with, make the choices not so simple. Muddy the waters just enough. I took another drink.

"Slow down Cheryl, you have all night and I doubt you want to wake with a hangover." he said still chuckling to himself. "How did you find me so easy? It takes the others forever to figure out where I am?" I asked actually interested in the difference. "Shop talk, rule number one remember?" he said and stood. I thought, well I've offended him again. That was fast.

Instead he put his hand out to me and almost on cue a slower song came on over the super speaker system. I thought I saw Juan give the DJ a thumbs up with his other hand and he guided me to the dance floor. His hand felt so warm on my back, it spread to places a girl doesn't talk about. How long had it been since someone touched me without trying to kill me? I reached out with my senses for some reason. Just a hunch and I felt nothing. Just regular people, but I knew Juan wasn't human, or at the very least, not any more. Why didn't he register? He guided me like a professional dancer around the floor. Maybe it was the rush of the drink but I wanted to kiss him again. Then it felt like someone threw water on me. I was dancing with a known demon, which by his very nature would have to try and kill me one day. What the hell was I doing? I broke the grip he had on me. I think I singed his hand as I pulled it from my back but I didn't turn around to see. I got out of there before my libido decided it was worth the risk. I know he was just behind me. I didn't need to look back to see that. When I got into my car I looked anyway and he didn't look hurt, or even angry. Still with that stupid smile on his face. I drove in circles, I doubt it would do any good if he found me so easy before, but why be stupid and just guess that he had a way to track me. By the time I got to the flea bag motel, I realized I was crying. He's a demon for Christ sake, not some bad boy biker, or Wall Street predator. It didn't matter. I cried anyway. I don't remember the last time I really cried. I made up for it this time though. Self-pity, anger, fear, and every other emotion I had been bottling up were piling up for their chance to pour from my eyes and out of my continuous wailing mouth in a steady stream of curse words.

When I woke up, I didn't have a hangover, but did have a sinus headache from crying so much. I needed to snap out of it. I took a shower. The water hit me mid neck level; I had to bend over just to wash my hair. I grudgingly took two of the suspect hotel towels and dried my hair and body, then wiped the mirror. I knew my eyes would be puffy, my face splotchy, I wasn't prepared for Juan's face looking back at me like a TV set. "RUN." he mouthed. No sound came out but it didn't have to. This part I was good at. I grabbed my clean clothes threw them on, grabbed my purse, the staff, and my mini bag of clothes and toiletries and hurtled out the door. I left the room key on the bed. Just as I climbed in my car throwing everything but the staff in the back seat I felt out and knew why I was running. There were Scions everywhere. On the roof, behind the hotel, in adjoining rooms. It was like a swat team, if a swat team could rip a roof off with their bare hands.

I peeled out of the parking as fast as the gravel would let my little super car. I was in fourth gear by the time I hit the pavement. I looked in my rear view and saw the normally bipedal Scions bounding like great dogs on all fours trying to match my speed. The first part of my plan worked,

get them away from innocents. The Second part
was yet to be determined. I had to find a way
to get out of here and out of their sight. The
word mix-master popped in my head and I went
straight into the middle of Dallas/Fort Worth.
I changed interstates three times crossing too
many lanes to count. Traffic wasn't bad, of course
this was the Deep South and it was Sunday. I got
to where I couldn't feel them anymore behind
me and watched as the road signs ticked by for
mileage to Las Vegas. I wasn't about to go near
that place and get people hurt. I knew it was
stupid, I knew I should avoid it. I headed for Death
Valley. If I had all of hell after me I was going to
take it to somewhere they couldn't hide. Desert,
even with the dunes, wasn't the treetops. They
would have to come at me and give me a chance to
take them out at a distance. If I was going to die,
it would be just me and on my terms. I sure as hell
wasn't going to make it easy for them.

CHAPTER TWENTY-NINE

I drove as fast as the local police would let me, I think I almost got pulled over once, but the officer was looking down at something when I flew past. I guess being on the good side had its benefits. I kept a constant scan going to make sure I wasn't headed into an ambush of Scions. I looked up into the mirror to see how bad I looked before heading into the gas station. The brown hair made my pale complexion stand out more. I tried to run my fingers through my hair. I knew better than to wash freshly colored hair. I wasn't thinking, my hands came away slightly Brown. Well crap, it wasn't coming off either. I untucked my shirt to give myself a more forgettable appearance and walked with my head lower like I was shy. I rummaged for food; I was starved and running low on money, no ten dollar bag of beef jerky for me this time. I grabbed some chips and a soda and headed to pay for my gas.

I think I was doing OK until I went to pay for the stuff and the gas. The small darker complected cashier looked at my hand as I handed him the money, then looked at my other hand. There was a moment of an eye lock. I could see the wheels turning as he was subtracting the brown from my hair in his head. "Thank you ma'am, come back soon." he said but it seemed automatic. Then he reached for a book under the counter. I could see him as I was pumping the gas; I noticed face drawings and pictures on the pages as he flipped them. Of course I would get Barney Fife for a convenience store clerk in the middle of nowhere. I got the gas topped off before he found what he was looking for; I was out of the parking lot and headed the wrong way on purpose. I drove about a mile then found a place to turn around and head back to the interstate. I figure if he had made me for the Sequoia fire, it was better that he said I took off east. I alternated between highway and side roads when the new sat-nav showed something promising. Running in terror makes your mind do funny things. Like driving hundreds of miles and not noticing a huge sat-nav on the dashboard. I figure if anyone was looking for me they would expect me to take the shortest distance. Bugs Bunny, I tell ya.

I hit the state line and got back on the interstate. I kept it exactly five miles an hour over the limit so I looked like every other car on the road. I tried to blend in, The flashing blue and reds told me I didn't do well enough. I sat in a too bright beam of light with my registration and insurance card ready. The officer finally made it up to me and said the famous cop phrase, "Do ya know why ah pulled ya over ma'am?" with such a draw in his voice I don't think he could have been more southern. I looked up and did my best Bambi impression, batting eyelashes, pouty lip, slightly arched back, "No officer what did I do wrong?"

I said. "Do ya know yer tags er outta date?"
he said looking at my ID and insurance card. I
wanted to smack myself in the head; I had been
running from place to place for a year. I hadn't
even thought about my plates expiring. Then he
shuffled the stuff I handed him. I knew this was
it, he was going to call it in and that would be all
she wrote. My heart sank; I tried to think but my
brain just made the sound from touching the side
in a game of operation. He flipped my registration
over. "Ma'am, seems like you just fergot ta put
the stickers on yer tags, they're still stapled ta the
paper." I blinked. I knew that wasn't right but I
was in no position to be right.

Dumb act in three, two, one. "Oh, I didn't know
what to do with them. My boyfriend always took
care of it for me. We broke up a while ago and I
totally had no idea." then I did the twisting my
hair thing. He looked at my hands, my hair, and
seemed to draw some conclusion in his head. He
handed back everything except the stickers, "I
will put these on for you so you don't get held
up anymore, and if you have any trouble with
someone on your way through." he handed me his
business card with his cell number scrawled on
the back. "Once I get these on, yer free ta go." he
said and stepped to the rear of the car bending to
apply the stickers.

I couldn't believe this, I knew things had just
happened for me, but this was stretching things. I

had no idea where the new tag stickers had come from but he obviously thought my bad dye job and mention of an ex made him think I was running from an abusive relationship. I guess running from the Scions put off the same vibe, but I was back on the road. No complaints here.

I was about ten miles down the road and Juan just appeared in the passenger seat with my staff between us. I guess I was getting used to this, I didn't even swerve lanes. "That was close; it's a good thing that the DMV got your new registration delivered in time." He flashed that grin that melted my everything. "Was that you? How did you? Never mind, I don't want to know. Do I have you to thank for this too?" I pointed at the sat-nav on my dash. "I bet you did the cabin paperwork at Sequoia too." I saw something new on his face, confusion, flustered, maybe some anger thrown in for good measure. "I was busy while you played in the woods. That is the only time I have been busy in the last year though." That left me confused. Juan didn't do it; nothing in heaven would have missed the official records.

"Oh Cheryl, I have been around more than you know to make sure no one cheats the future. Just not while you were in California." He said plainly. He used my name again, it sounded almost like a musical note when he said it. No one used my name like that in over a year. All the Demon's Scions called me Sprite, and Father Ryan and the occasional desk clerk at the motel called me Angel. I had been careful not to get close to anyone and only told three people my name since this started. I knew none of them told anyone. "Why do you call me Cheryl, when the others call me Sprite or Angel?" I asked doing my best to stare straight ahead. "I believe in using the proper name for things, you are neither Angel nor a true Sprite. You are not wholly human either. You are Cheryl." he said with another music note on my name. He paused for effect and then for the first time offered an answer for something I hadn't asked yet. "You know that the Scions are close to immortal, to them it has only been a few blinks of time since Seraphim walked the earth. They called the Seraphim Sprite. Some of the others have been around for so long they only remember the Angels. The Angels have been around but also can sense your true nature. You are as close to a Sprite as this planet will see but to me it doesn't cover who you are as well as Cheryl." he finished with one last pluck of the note. Now he was doing it on purpose.

I did note the difference in his and Father Ryan's explanation. Father Ryan made sure to emphasize Amon just enough, Juan didn't even bother to mention him. "But you took me to see Hell, I felt the evil creep over you when we kissed. Doesn't that kind of put you on the other side of this?" I asked thoroughly confused. "I am many things, and I have had many names, but neither side may claim me for their own. Let us just agree that I am a balance." he said simply. I could tell that was all I was getting out of him about himself. "Why me though?" I asked the question that had been driving me nuts for a year now. "If not you, who would you choose to take your place and risk their life, and the lives of every creature on this planet should they fail?" he folded his hands into his lap knowing this was going to be a long mental task. I imagined a dozen action heroes from the movies. I played with this game for fifteen or twenty miles.

By the time I was accepting that I really wouldn't wish this on anyone else, he held out his hands like he had read my mind. "That is precisely why you." then he was gone, just like that. I was really getting sick of this coming and going when they wanted but if I wanted anything I had to scream their name. Seemed like it was all one sided. Juan wasn't Angel or Demon, he must have been really old to have all that in his head. He spoke like they were memories. How old do you have to be to remember Demons fighting Angels and the great flood? My head hurt trying to work all of this out. I reached the last gas station before I would be heading into desert. I went inside to get gas and just skipped the chips this time knowing how low I was on cash. Getting stranded in the desert without water and gas was a bad idea no matter who you were. I walked up with the water and went to pay for the gas; there was a small stack of twenties and two fifties where I previously had ones. I acted like I just forgot something and went back for several more bottles of water and a pack of jerky. I could get used to this appearing money thing. If it wasn't for the constant dread, the imminent evisceration, not to mention putting up with the smell of the Scions, this would be pretty fun.

I headed out to the desert chewing on a piece of beef jerky and listening to music. The music gave out first. Guess I was outside of cellphone range, yup, no bars. Then I started giving out, I was dead tired. I didn't like the idea of sleeping in my car when I had no idea how far away the Scions and their masters were. I didn't know if physical space really meant that much or they just couldn't find me so easily. I had no idea if they were an hour behind me or a day. I just knew they were coming. The car suddenly got a little cooler inside even though I had turned the engine off, losing my air conditioning. I reached out fearing the worst, instead I felt like I was surrounded by the lightest feelings, not the sliminess of the Scions. I barely had time to register that I was safe for now before I was asleep drooling on my seat.

CHAPTER THIRTY

I woke up with a very different feeling. It was much warmer; I was half covered in sweat even though the sun had barely broken the horizon. I rubbed my eyes and stretched. I felt something really close, it was as dark as a tar pit and just as slimy, I heard a crunch and the sound of metal shredding from the roof, there was no sense of lightness nearby, the sun was rising but it was like a huge cloud was descending over the whole area. My right hand hit my staff and I grabbed it as I dove out of the car door. There were five here, they weren't even trying to hide. There was nothing but sand, this area was very flat with the dunes in the distance. The one on my roof was another of the white haired scions. Maybe they were the equivalent to hunting dogs for them. I spun the rod as I felt the lines of power leading back to the hooded man in the back. A row of black spikes protruded from the hood. If that didn't give you nightmares nothing would.

The tendrils of power reached out from the spiked demon to each of the four white haired Scions. I noticed that they weren't circling like they usually would. They didn't like direct confrontations. That's fine I didn't need to turn to see when they were flanking me now. The ground felt like an oil stain was directly under all four of them. The tendrils were just a good backup in case they suddenly leapt at me. Something wasn't right though. The controlling demon with the spikes didn't have the same dark oil slick feel. In the woods against the MegaScion, I noticed the dark feeling of the controlling demon. What was different this time?

"Angel, you have no reason to run today." the voice just over a rasp but perfectly audible even from this distance. I looked at the demon, never letting my guard down in case it was a ploy to get the Scions into place. "Tell that to my car." I yelled back. I know it is just a car, but it was one of the last things I had from my life before all of this started. "You're Amon, right? The one that suddenly decided to turn my life upside down." I waited, the Scions were perfectly still like statues. If I risked to look directly at one of them, I had the impression they would be like statues, unblinking, not twitching. It was creepier than the way they moved. I kept my eyes fixed on Amon. "You are not here by accident, you are here because it is your time to be here." he said still raspy, like the hood made plain speech impossible. "Sorry I missed that fortune cookie, but I got the one that said you will find good luck where you least expect it." I was so through being scared of these monsters. I heard a raspy caw sound and realized after a moment that he was laughing. Were demons allowed to have a sense of humor? It kind of goes against the whole bastions of darkness vibe they love. "You still have much time left or you don't, for this luck you were promised." great I have a spiky Yoda for an arch-enemy. "Let me guess, all it cost is my soul right? I heard that was a big thing where you call home. Am I supposed to kneel before your throne for all eternity and count my fortunes while roasting?" This did something finally. "That isn't my reason; the souls are for the collectors." He straightened to an impressive height. Wearing the cloak and hood I hadn't realized how much he was hunched over. He had to be seven foot tall. OK, so a little intimidating.

"What do you know of your pursuer? Do you know his name? His purpose? Would you recognize him anywhere?" Now I was confused, "Aren't you the one hunting me with your hounds and other assorted meat heads?" Again with the crazy laugh caw thing. The Scions still didn't move. That was a plus, but could lure me into a false sense of security. "Is it these that you call hounds?" he said gesturing at the Scions. I just nodded without taking my eyes off him. I jumped back as red flames ignited each of them as fast as my blue-white fire could have and ashes hit the ground. This wasn't good, if this Amon wanted to attack me, I am pretty sure I would be dust before I knew he was attacking. I needed to start thinking of an exit strategy and not piss him off at the same time. "What do you want with me then? I am just a girl trying to get some kind of normal life back." I said taking a tentative step back. He didn't move but we were still the same distance apart. "What do you know of me, Angel?" he asked. "From everything I found, you are the one who knows things in the future and past, high up in the throne count, and have at least ten different descriptions of your 'reason'. You make sure things come out in your bosses favor when you can. That doesn't mean you aren't evil, or wanting to kill me." I said forgetting to be afraid of him. "If it was your time to die and it was to be by my hand, you would, I have told you from my own mouth that I am not here to kill you. You are correct you have a choice, but it doesn't involve your soul. You give me your answer and we are done." he ended as if this explained everything. "Answers require a question, if I have a choice give it to me or go play on your throne." I said. I was so frustrated and bone tired I didn't even care anymore who he thought he was. "Who has turned their hand to you, and to what end? You should have all you need to know from the Other." he rasped again quieter. The Other? What the hell is the Other? He said it like a title, not like he was talking about someone generically.

If he thought I had all the information, I had the impression that he was right. Demon or not, he hadn't done more than get my attention and talk. So far every experience I had with Demon's and Scion's involved the visceral urge to kill me. I tried to think. I didn't know many people involved, there was Juan who definitely knew how to track me and had raged at me, there was this supposed Demon Belial that I knew little about except his title, the Prince of Lies. There were the ArchAngels that seemed to be there when I got in over my head. They definitely weren't it. So this guy Belial or Juan was the one after me. If it was Juan though, he had proven to be able to track me no matter how well I hid. I wouldn't have had months in the Sequoias or in Tennessee. So it had to be this Demon Belial, but he hadn't shown his face once that I knew of. The ArchAngel basically told me it was Belial, but that was too easy. This Amon thing wouldn't ask me for something I had already been told. Trying to do the mental gymnastics of applied algebra to a word problem. I think I wanted a scratch piece of paper. There was something nagging at me. Something I had missed in all the confusion. It wasn't something that was there, but not there when it should have been. When it clicked, it was the only thing that made sense. If Amon did know the future and the way things needed to play out, he would have known what Juan the not-demon had shown me. That another Demon was trying to usurp a higher throne. Belial was counted as lower than Amon, I had seen both thrones. Belial's Scions were the white hairs. That is the what I saw gathered in front of his throne. The only time the tendrils of power seemed to connect them, was when one Demon was using the other's Scions. The MegaScion weren't white hairs, they were the smarter more human like ones. I bet if some of them showed up, Amon wouldn't need to control them directly because they would do whatever he wanted. That meant, only one thing I met made sense. He wasn't there after I beat the spiked Scions in Tennessee.

"Father Ryan is his disguise. He is the one hunting me and trying to take your throne." I said confident in the logic, but feeling sick after trusting in him so much. I was reliant on him. He gave me the Bible I needed; he was concerned when I lost the Rod of Moses, gas money, everything for half a year. I wish I wasn't so certain. My stomach actually ached at the thought. Amon's cowl dropped and back up in an apparent nod. "It is time you left Angel. You have an appointment to keep." he said and was gone. I reached out to see if I could find him, expecting a trap. You don't trust demons, no matter how well-mannered they seem. I knew that much, they could thank you as they gutted you. The one thing that convinced me he was really gone was thinking of his purpose in being here at all. Self-interest, if Belial wanted his throne and Amon wasn't ready to just hand it over, He would be on my side for this. The thought of having a demon on my side didn't sit well with my dinner from the night before. There was another niggling feeling that wasn't sitting right. Why did I feel like I had Angelic protection just in the place where a demon would pop up seven hours later? It wasn't like the Demons and Angels were texting buddies.

I walked to my now partially convertible baby. It wasn't too bad as long as I didn't wreck it. The hole just looked like a can opener got to the driver side roof. I got in and started her up. "Good girl" I said as I patted the dash. I started to drive off slowly to not kick up dust or get stuck getting back on the road. That is when I felt them. The slimy group that had attacked me in Tennessee, the ones that attacked in California. All of the ones left were here. The car dug in for a second and then caught traction. I could almost claim whiplash from the change in speed. I had said Father Ryan's name talking to Amon, that was how they knew where to find me. I almost bought a convertible instead of my Mini, I was glad I hadn't as the air from highway speeds was whipping my hair and stinging my face. Random paper bags flew out from the drive here. The Scions and Belial were all still converging on where I had been. So it worked like a ping. He knew where I was when I said either of his names. That was good information, if I only knew what I was going to do with it or where I was headed.

CHAPTER THIRTY-ONE

I guess saying I was through running was a bit of an overstatement. Technically I had no idea where I was going yet. So was that running or just being lost with speed? I hit Vegas and had to decide quickly which way to go. I was going to head back east but some jerk in an over-sized SUV made the choice for me. I hated those things; even more I hated the drivers who were oblivious to everything around them. I drove faster and slower for a half a mile trying to get over. He just stayed talking into his phone right beside me. There was too much traffic to do something stupid like slam on the brakes. Besides I was still wanted around here. Couldn't go throwing up more red flags beyond my screwed up roof. I merged north instead.

I guess I was headed in the right direction. The ride became more peaceful and uneventful. If I was headed where I thought I was, I would need to fix the roof somehow. I didn't have time for a good body shop, so I settled for some duct tape with little mustaches on it. It did the trick for now keeping the worst of the wind out. It definitely gave me time to think. If this Amon thing wanted me to stop Not-Father Ryan, I was going to need a plan. One that didn't end with me dead. I thought about my desert strategy and saw the flaws with that scenario. If they rushed me on the flat ground I had nowhere to go. If he brought the MegaScion with him, I could be in real trouble without something to help the impact along. I needed to think strategically. The woods and urban settings were completely indefensible, due to the Scion's propensity for climbing and dropping on prey. Flatland was out too, they could just hoard rush me. I needed something with a good advantage. Like a hill or even better a mountain. I wasn't far from Colorado; they have a bunch of mountains that are uninhabited. I set the sat-nav to Denver. I figure it's the mile high city they had to have some big mountains there. My knowledge of Colorado was limited but I did know the major mountains were there.

I drove for a while on autopilot, how I didn't wreck I am not sure. I am still not completely sure I didn't fall asleep for a quarter-mile of particularly straight and flat road. I finally started going uphill when I was in Utah. It was beautiful. The red rock outcroppings everywhere, the old style homes with the clay tile roofs and stucco walls. If I got through all this I was going to have to come back here just to look around and take it all in at a lower speed. The air was still loud rushing past the taped roof and it was getting cooler. Oh, how I wished for someone to magically fix my roof the way they did before. I know it is childish and I don't care. It was important to me. Before I could mentally put my hands on my hips in defiance at the injustice of freezing, I felt the car warming and then Juan was seated next to me, He was wearing a blue tank top that showed his muscular arms well, too well. I am not sure what changed but he looked like some kind of model now. His face angular in contrast with his skin color, rather European in bone structure, but a Mexican or Mayan skin tone. He reminded me of a college trip to Cozumel we took. The waiters all had that look. Like next week was their cover shoot for GQ or something. He wore rather tight blue jeans that said he cared about his appearance. Not everyone goes around with creases in their jeans.

 "So, where are we headed now Cheryl?" it was a simple question. I remained guarded though, if Father Ryan wasn't who he appeared then I couldn't trust my eyes when it came to any of them, nor did I have an idea of their true intentions. "Just headed north, what about you? Why are you here?" I looked at Juan for too long and a wolf or big coyote ran in front of my car. I swerved to avoid it and nearly flipped us over. In the quick flash of my life up until now something registered, Juan's face had subtly changed since the first time I met him. Like I saw what he wanted me to see, or what I wanted to see. That was a little more than disconcerting. So far nothing was what it seemed to be. My neighbor with the greasy hair was an ArchAngel, Father Ryan was a demon, the Scions could walk around a mall when they wanted, and now Juan could look like what he chose.

He could sense something was wrong. His posture got straighter, his manner more abrupt. "You will need to find something better than a mountain Cheryl. Look for something that makes sense. Look for what has stood the test of time like the Angels. It is where you need to be. I can't help you fight; all I can do is keep things equal. He has power and an army. You have your guile and powers you haven't even tapped into yet. If you find it and get there ahead of him. He will fall, I have seen it already. If not then there is nothing more I can do. I will see you one way or the other after." With that he was gone. It was still warm in the car, not as drafty. I looked up and the roof was whole again. I guess if nothing else my Juan, the balance dude was a hell of a car repair wizard. I finally had to stop just inside a small town near one of the salt lakes. It wasn't large, but the hotels were nicer than the one in Tennessee. I went to check into my room, exhausted, but glad for the chance to stretch my legs. I didn't even realize I was in trouble until it was too late. Two Scions, the white hairs were on me in a moment's notice of getting out of the car. I grabbed my staff on reflex getting out of the car. If I hadn't, I would not be here to tell my story. I managed to block one as the other sank a single claw into my side like a scalpel. I could feel the weight of a cracked rib against my lung making breathing harder, not that it was easy to breath after such a change in elevation. I tried to hit several with fire but they stayed out of the reach of that and my staff. As all four lined up around me I had an inspiration. If my Juan was right and I had powers I hadn't tapped into yet, maybe my Staff had some mystical powers like the Staff of Moses, just maybe I could use one of the attacks in a similar method. I waited until they were all settled in position to strike. I felt the first one get ready to spring into a charge and unleashed a ground strike that sent ripples of pavement in every direction. I could feel the inky blackness beneath each of them draw the ripples their way like iron drawn to a magnet. Then just poof, they were gone, dust in the wind they were just ash floating as the blue-white fire consumed them. I reached out for the next set but they weren't there. They must have been a forward unit to find me. There weren't any more near but I knew I was on the right trail.

I spent the rest of the duct tape and gauze I had left on my rib and the cut over it. Breathing was difficult but I eventually found a position that was at least tolerable. Thank goodness for free ice in the hotel. Once I was settled in my room I tried to figure out what Juan meant by his cryptic "help". Somewhere ancient that made sense. I had no clue. I started going through the maps but they were no help. It is a big freaking country. I finally gave up figuring it out and passed out from exhaustion.

When I woke it was time for the free breakfast. I didn't want to miss that. Free was good. I was soaking wet from the ice bags turned waterspouts on my bed. I'm sure it wasn't the worst thing they ever cleaned up but I made sure to leave a tip anyway. I walked through the lobby and got my food. I sat at a fairly clean table. Just some junk pamphlets left by tourists. I ate and read about the Grand Canyon. Then the last one was for a place I had never been.

CHAPTER THIRTY-TWO

I drove a little further up the road to a cheaper hotel. Sitting in one spot wasn't a great idea with people around. It was warm inside my room and I slept like a baby the second night after planning all day. I am sure it was a false sense of security, but I knew none of the Scions would attack me tonight. Maybe word got back that I killed two at once. More likely there was someone watching over me. That was reinforced when I walked to my car, forgetting my coat, and didn't shiver to death in the cold air. This wasn't one of the nice hotels where they served breakfast; it was probably no better than the fleabag motel in Tennessee, but it had a feeling of safety to it. My dark auburn hair was already starting to fade to a pinkish color. It would be strawberry again soon where I washed it the most. I am sure I wouldn't attract any attention with pink shoulder length hair. When I went to get the gas I realized that maybe it wasn't so bad of a disguise after all. The girl at the register had bright blue hair that I am sure didn't mean she was from Mars. It seemed a cultural norm around here to have off color hair. Plus one to society for that, I would still have to be careful. I knew there were Scions around but they all seemed at a safe distance. Like they were tracking me but were afraid to actually try to tree me. I pulled out my money and the same trick as before; the ones and fives were replaced with fifties and twenties. I already made twice as much in the last year than I would have at my accounting job. I hit I-70 and kept going toward Denver it was a long drive but felt a little safer than the direct root. I didn't need them to figure out where I was headed and have days to set up. I started having images in my head of the battle. I could see me on top of a huge monument with them all scrambling to get up to me. Just picking them off one by one like some carnival game. If I was picking off the Scion's though who would take out Belial?

I had no idea how to get to the top, it's not like they had an elevator or something built into the rock facing, but I would figure that out when I got there. I was worn out, I needed a place to stay and needed to keep myself rested, fed, and ready to deal with them or it would be over fast. I pictured the last moments of a slow fly just as he was going to get swatted. Shook my head and kept driving. Grand Junction in twenty three miles. That would have to be it for now. I came this way before when I ended up in Yellowstone. I knew there wasn't much between here and Denver. I did the scanning thing and couldn't find any Scions but I was getting less and less comfortable with my ability to sense them. It was like they adapted so I couldn't find them so easy the last few times I had them nearby. They gave up hiding when they were on top of me but if they were a few cars behind me I am sure they didn't want me to know.

They loved their surprises more than a kid at a carnival.

I decided to try something different as I got into town, instead of looking for a dark space, I looked for light. There seemed to be something to the north of the town. Maybe I was finally getting some help besides cryptic words and time bending handymen. I found the hotel it was coming from, it was one of the bigger chains. I usually avoided them, but I felt like this was where I was meant to be.

I checked in pretty easily for someone paying cash, not my usual experience of credit card only that they normally mandated. Guess I was less of a threat than an out of state rock band. They hadn't seen my last few rooms obviously. I went up to the third floor went in the room and stripped quickly. Oh freedom thy name is no bra straps. I looked at the literature on the table. There were the usually pamphlets about room service etc. and one that mentioned the sauna. A real sauna, with heat, and moisture, and muscle rending goodness. They had a pool but I was less interested in that. They had a small store too. I needed a new swim suit, The Scions at Yellowstone had seen to that. I called down and they had a full supply of swimwear. I guess that wasn't something most people packed when they headed to the mountains.

I grabbed a new toothbrush, some cream eggs for later and began suit hunting. The one piece rack was all way too short for me. So I reluctantly looked for the two piece racks. I didn't like two piece suits; I liked the ones with the ruffled skirts on the bottoms so you didn't feel so exposed. Then to my horror the only thing that actually fit me was white. I was definitely not swimming in that one. But I wouldn't be swimming anyway but the horror of the idea still played out in my head. It even furnished the teenage gawkers and old leering men. I could throw a t-shirt over the top of it I guess. I saw the wolf like smile on the checkout clerks face and decided I was definitely not even going to set a single foot in the pool. He looked like a college student smelling pizza on finals week. If I had stayed around any longer he might have gotten up the courage to ask to go with me, or start humping my leg. Neither were up my alley, so I got out of there quick being sure to give him a fake room number a few doors down. I thought it was odd that he was asking since I was paying cash and not charging it to my room. The last thing I needed was him spying on me later in the evening. I went upstairs and changed into the bathing suit.

First I looked in the mirror. OK so a year of running and fighting had done me well in the love handle department, but I still felt like my mom was yelling at me to put some clothes on. I actually had some curves in the right places now. I wouldn't say I was a vain person but I would be lying if I said I didn't look at every angle to spot any problem areas I still needed to firm up. I threw a shirt over it and it hung to my mid-thigh. That would be fine if I didn't reach over my head for anything. I tested it and sure enough, you could see the duct tape and everything below it when I lifted my arms. I tried to wrap one of their towels around my waist but they were all too short. I grabbed two and made a small skirt of them. Tucked my key card in my waistband and headed down to the first floor with the sauna waiting for me.

I could tell someone else was in there because it was dark and hot already. I opened the door and sat down determined not to talk to anyone and just let it soak in. The wood seating was dry for maybe thirty seconds before I started soaking it with sweat. I did the neck rotations and tried to do some meditation to steady my breathing so I could stay in longer. The heat started drying and the young man with a scar across his face got up to pour more hot water on the glowing red rocks. It was Father Richardson.

I tried to figure out what brought him to this exact location and waiting for me in the sauna no less. I tried to strike up a conversation but my mouth wasn't cooperating. I decided to stick to short sentences. "What brings you out here?" I readied myself for the pause he applied to each answer. I didn't need to though, "I am here for you." He said it in a way that I normally associated with young, hormone driven youth. Definitely not something I expected from a pastor. "How did you know I was going to be here?" "A little birdy told me." Then he added, "You really shouldn't be so skittish, I'm only here to talk." I wanted to ask about the stammer, I wanted to ask about his lack of clothes. The only thing I could get out was "OK talk then." "Do you think it is hard to find you when you run so much, or do you just enjoy your new found freedom?" First I was struck by the calmness in his speech. The second thing was his attitude. It wasn't coming from a place of concern. It seemed to be another conversation and he was just continuing it. He still kept pouring water on the rocks making it uncomfortable. I wanted to say something but I couldn't let him see me worried. He didn't just have a smoother speaking voice, there was something familiar about his movements. He had a confident air to his posture as he was standing and pouring even more water on the glowing stones. He didn't have the meek attitude I saw in Huntsville. "What do you want from me? The church has already made its position on helping me very rigid." The corner of his mouth turned up into a smile. "Why would you think the church could do otherwise, Angel?"

My mind went dead for a minute, there wasn't just something off about his speaking and body language. He wasn't the same person. He called me Angel. No one did that except. "Father Ryan got to you didn't he? What did he promise, a stammer free voice and a chance with the ladies? I hate to be the one to break it to you but you still have zero chance here." I'm not sure if the change happened while I was talking or just directly after I finished. Instead of Father Reynolds standing there, Father Ryan was in his place. Every detail changed from his age to his difference in height. I tried to think about what I needed to do but before I could act, the door made a popping sound like it was barring itself from the outside. Father Ryan, still pouring water on the rocks with his back to me asked "is that warm enough Angel?" "Umm yeah that is fine." I answered dully; still shocked I hadn't sensed him. "You and I have a lot to discuss. I think you have the wrong impression of me."

I stood up trying the door but it wouldn't budge. I turned to look at him but he was still just as disinterestedly treating the coals. I started to get hot in ways that had nothing to do with the sauna. "I don't think you're going to like how this turns out for you if you don't let me leave." "If you think your powers will work right here, I am sure you would mean it, but I made a deal, and you have nothing here but your words, just as I don't. We are just two vanilla mortals having a conversation for the next thirty minutes. Sure enough I tried to vaporize the water in the bucket next to him and nothing. I had nothing at all. That would explain why I didn't feel him. "I don't see what you would have to say, that would change my mind in the least, everything lined up still has to happen." "Oh dear Angel, you have, what's the phrase, drank the Kool-Aid" I was shocked he would know such a recent slang, let alone how to use it. "Thirty minutes you say?" I asked. "Yes, then you're free to do what you want with me. My existence is numbered after this anyway, I am hoping for a larger number is all." he finished with a smile that was creepy and self-satisfied at the same time.

CHAPTER THIRTY-THREE

The steam kept billowing out from the rocks as Father Ryan poured more water over them. It was way past my comfort level, but I wasn't about to give him the satisfaction of knowing that. "So have you been having fun with your little game pretending to help me all this time?" I sneered as I sat back down. I don't know why, but I was sure that what he said was probably the first honest thing to leave his mouth. We had thirty minutes with no powers, thirty minutes to hear what the other might say. I knew I was dealing with Belial but I think he was at least more pleasant to look at as Father Ryan. "I have helped you, my goal was to get you to build on your powers so our goals were aligned. The fact that I did it in a former shell was just convenient." he replied without turning around. "Then who would you make a deal with on my behalf, to talk to you without powers? I am pretty sure everyone on my side of the fence wants to see me take you out." I said. He turned and sat in a very unflattering manner. Towel draped around his waist in such a way that it emphasized his gaunt midsection. His face still looked pudgy but his body was all flab and rolls. There were scars running from one side to the other in irregular patterns that could have only come from regular whipping. On any other person on this planet, it might have brought some sympathy. On him it made me smile to think there was indeed some justice even for creatures like him.

"What is there to talk about? You're a lying demon, I am the closest to a 'hands on' Angel, and someone has seen that we had thirty minutes to talk. Are you supposed to convince me not to destroy you at my first chance, are you going to tell me to join your side because it is so much fun to be bound like Father Richardson?" I asked. He didn't move his head at all, then said "You know that I am right, Amon is weak, and weakness is not in anyone's best interest. If Hell is weak, then there must be a balance. If there is to be a balance then one of the Angels must fall. Have you not given thought to your secondary use if you were to fail in eliminating Amon?" He asked then waited with a smile and a steepling of his hands as he waited for a response. The ArchAngels never said I was created to destroy Amon. It could be that he didn't know I was in contact with them at times.

I knew he was the one blasted back in the woods when I split the MegaScion from the controlling demon. He never knew of the time I spent talking to an ArchAngel. On his side of the fence it hadn't happened. I would have loved to see the look on his face. "If you believe I was created to slay Amon to bring balance back, why is it you, that has attacked me so regularly, why is it you, that seems to be hounding me, and why do you need to rope his Scions into servitude when yours have failed?" I asked. Then without waiting for an answer, "If Amon is who I think he is, then I can see why you are so afraid of him. The one to know the future and the past, the one to make sure your boss is well placed in the final battle. Why shouldn't it be you? You are a natural second to the king of lies, but you fear you will never get that position when the time of the great battle has begun." I finished and saw it had the desired effect of verbally slapping him.

His eyes were now black, all black; he looked more ferocious than one of his beasts. "You have no idea of the power that you are playing with little Angel. You are but a slip of power compared to what I hold and what I have seen. Do you not doubt that I can swat you like a small bug at any time? I want the same thing that your progenitor wants. Balance, we both need balance or the halving does not work. You were never made to be strong, you were made to be an offering of balance." he said with spit flying from the corner of his mouth. His features now bulging and slightly red from exertion as if he had run a flight of stairs. "So you're saying that I am here to remove Amon from power, so that you can step into his place because he is weak? You think I have just enough power to remove him. If I remove him what happens to me next? Do I die in the effort, do I go back to my normal life, or do I

spend the rest of eternity running from one attack
or another?" I asked truly curious what he would
say.

"I can make a pact that you are not to be
touched or molested in any way after I am in
power. It is much more than Amon would even do.
He has been a general for so long he forgets that
sometimes mutually beneficial pacts are useful. He
only sees war that has yet to be. On the final days
of course all pacts will be gone and the battle will
be truly be glorious. I am sure you will have a part
to play as well that way." he finished with a smile.
Did he just admit that I was going to be around for
the final days? I didn't know if that meant they
were close at hand or if I would live longer than
I should. The ArchAngel said I had the frailties
of humans. Wouldn't that mean I should expect
to die in a traditional lifetime. I was beginning
to doubt anything these supernatural types told
me. None of them came out and just said stuff.
Everything was wrapped in doublespeak. I vaguely
wondered what level of shock that would cause
to poor Maureen. She put all of her eggs in one
basket so to speak.

I tried to figure out how long we had been in
here, fifteen, twenty minutes. I think I had an idea
what he thought was going on, as well as what
my real reason was now, but I had to let this play
out and I needed to stall for time. "You never
answered the first thing I asked, that is important

if you want me to believe that you only want what is best for both sides. Who did you make this deal with that can strip our powers, make us mortal even temporarily? The ArchAngels have never seen a use for you or your words; I know that the Demons don't have any power over my abilities. You aren't going to tell me that they just decided to get these two love birds together for old time sake and let bygones be bygones. So who was it? Simple question, and your running out of time." I finished.

Was it twenty five minutes now. I had to get an answer out of him. I knew every word he said was laced with lies, you don't get to be the Prince of Lies telling people things straight out, but maybe I could figure out this mess by the lie he chose. "Oh you know the Other. They are as old as this battle and they have a great need to see that the sides are in an alignment. So much that they would sacrifice anything to see it happen. It is their nature. Harmony dictates it, and Harmony it shall have."

He was talking about Juan. I should be mad at Juan, but something in me snapped. I caught the old priest off guard with a punch to the face. He rocked back and laughed. Blood dribbling from his mouth and laughing looked wrong on anyone. Psycho wrong. I went for a second hit the blood pumping through my body so hard I was shaking with each beat of my heart. This time the old priest was ready for it and spun my arm to the side. He tried to get a lock on me but I managed to avoid my arm dislocating with a rotation of my hips. I put pressure back on his arms instead of mine and popped him in the ear as hard as I could. I didn't want to get into a grappling match with a demon, even without his powers he had centuries of knowledge. The best I could do was act like a boxer, hit him and get out of the way before he could turn the advantage. "Did I tell you something you didn't want to hear? I don't want to be the one to tell you, but you were made to be hurt." Father Ryan said through globs of blood coming from his mouth now. "I just enjoy finally having a target, I hope you don't mind the severe beating I am going to give you." I said as I spun a kick towards his unprotected testicles. I missed the kick but only by a little. His leg snapped out when I hit the right thigh causing him to be thrown off balance. I reached back for another hit and could feel the power building inside me but tried to keep it from showing. I didn't want Father Ryan to know time was up if he hadn't already felt it. I tried to keep my face icy as I built up a full strike right to his face. Just as I was about to release it though. "Sorry Angel, You won't be needing that today." and he was gone.

He was lying again. I felt the outside of the Sauna surrounded by darkness. There were more of the Scions around pacing and stalking toward the barred door. The entire thing was a setup. I knew these were all hounds of Belial's; I knew he wouldn't be commanding any more of Amon's Scions anytime soon. No dark tethers to track them with but I could still feel the greasy stain under their feet.

I took all the energy that I had built up and struck down with it. I felt it rush back up in bursts at all of the greasy spots outside of the sauna. The door opened as easy as if it had never been stuck closed. I ran out and tagged three more that were in mid leap when I had sent out the first burst and turned them to ash. I could feel something behind me and spun just in time to catch one flying at my back, claws raised to strike. I threw out my hands to push her away. And a gust of wind pushed her back so hard she crunched on the metal railing for the second floor and nearly wrapped around it. The wind power could be just as useful, but nothing beat a good cleansing of fire. For good measure I burnt her to ash, I had seen these things re-knit themselves and jump back into a fight before. I wasn't going to take that risk again. Two more tried the wolf pack approach of splitting away to attack my rear when the other was running away. Bad habits are hard to break I guess. I struck the ground with my foot and the ground rose like a wave of fire at the two behind me and did my best impersonation of a bull fighter, avoiding the claws and teeth of the one in front of me sending him into the concrete wall like a water balloon. Then I sent out a wave of fire from both sides at the same time just as more tried to line up. Walla "Anyone order flame broiled Scions?" I shouted.

I didn't have to play these games anymore. I was done being afraid of them. I took determined steps to the stairs blasting each one that felt stupid enough to get close. The last two tried to come down on me from the third floor balcony. I shot both of them back in the air and fried them while they were at the mercy of gravity. More ash like snow fell.

My whole body radiated heat. I felt like I was still in the sauna. I looked down and realized I was covered from head to toe with a blue-white flame and my back was killing me. Did one of them get a hit in and I missed it? I felt around for more of them but the place was clean now. I guess Belial was bad at underestimating me or he was holding back for a big strike later. The latter was probably true. I looked around and the place was thankfully empty. Middle of the week guests must turn in early. I let the fire die down with some careful breathing and relaxing thoughts.

I reached for my door key and it wasn't there, worse, neither was my embarrassing white swimsuit. I don't think I have run so fast in my life to get back into a sauna. I saw on the floor were the two towels I had brought with me, they wouldn't quite cover, but it was better than nothing. After picking them up I saw the little plastic card underneath. I breathed a sigh of relief. I wouldn't be forced to go to the front desk dressed like this to get another key. I tried to tie them in a make shift, old dinosaur movie Raquel Welch outfit. One draped across my chest tucked into the bottom that left hanging points like half a dress covering my modesty. The other thing missing was the duct tape, and the wound it had been covering. Just like that, no more broken rib, no more cut. I took in a deep breath just as a means to test it. Everything was in place.

I moved as fast as the outfit would allow me to and made it back towards my room. I realized too late why no one was in the courtyard. I stepped up the darkened hallway. I saw what was left of a man partially bisected in the walkway. Behind him I saw doors open, and more bodies some having never got out of bed. The light that I felt when I came here was gone. I couldn't feel a single presence other than my own. I wanted to be sick, There didn't seem to be any rhyme or reason to this, why kill so many people. Why would anything do this? It wasn't just a slaughter, it was a senseless one. I got back to my room shaking. It was like the scene in Huntsville and in every nightmare I had since then. It was all I could do to get dressed and get my stuff together. My hands were shaking like I was suffering a seizure.

I was terrified, but more than that I was mad. If Belial wanted a fight he had one. He made a huge mistake giving me the lay of the land the way he did. I knew who all the players were now, I knew who my target was, and he was going to pay for each and every one of these people's lives. I would make sure that Belial would regret both massacres before I completely erased him. The surprise I had lined up for him was going to rock his flabby jowls. I looked in the mirror as I headed toward Denver and saw blue-white flames in my eyes. That made me smile, he was done, whether he knew it or not.

CHAPTER THIRTY-FOUR

I tried to make it to Denver in record time. My stomach didn't agree though. I pulled over so often to be sick every time the vision of another mutilated person popped into my brain, that it took a ridiculous amount of time to get there. I tried to focus on the here and now, my plan, but the reasons I needed to do this were woven into each part so tightly that I couldn't just separate them. The Scions at Belial's disposal were little more than feral beings with little thought of their own. The time that we were in the sauna, he had no control over them. I had also figured out that the Scions were a reflection of the demon they followed. Belial was pure reaction, Prince of lies; he had no other way to be. Amon was cunning and manipulative but didn't move unless it was advantageous. I wondered if this plan worked, what would happen to what was left of Belial's Scions, would they cease to be, or just get absorbed into another demon's service. I guess I would have to figure that out after I got rid of this slime ball.

"Juan, I could use you here right now." I half shouted into the emptiness of the car. I had more of a temper going than I meant to. I waited to call Juan just to give myself time to calm down. It didn't work. He was sitting there before I even finished my sentence. "Did I really need to see that? Is that what you call balance, tons of dead people who were innocent bystanders?" He sat for a moment and didn't say anything. I started making a growling sound unconsciously. When he spoke, it was somewhat softer than I was used to from him. He didn't wear his normal devil may care grin. His brow was furrowed and his lips were firmly set in a grimace. "I only allowed what the demon proposed, A peaceful summit meeting, He is the one who saw it as another advantage and unleashed his hell things there. He knew what they would do if he was cut off, and yet the idea of getting to you early was worth defying the purpose of the request."

He took a breath but started speaking again in a long fluid monologue. "The one thing you have to remember from now until time ends, Demons are to their nature as much as Angels are to theirs. If an Angel has the character of helping even when they shouldn't, they will. If a Demon has the character to lie, they will. They are not humans with ranges. For the Demons as well as the Angels now, everything is black and white. You are the only gray area that isn't purely human now." He finished much louder than he had started. "OK, so if you aren't an Angel, and you aren't a Demon, where do you fall on this black and white line Mr. Balance?" I asked, nearly spitting out the last words and feeling cheated somehow. He always skirted the "Who are you really?" questions since I had met him on that beach. Now that I had a good idea, I should probably be scared shitless, but I was so tired of the nearly constant lying to get me to do stuff, I didn't care enough to be scared. "I fall exactly where you know I do, in the middle, if there is too much from the darker sides, I do what I can to help the lighter and the other way around." he said as if he were explaining a simple concept. "So you're telling me you help these demons, you help the bastards that kill innocent people just for checking in to the wrong motel?" I was breathing hard like I was running, my pulse was spiking and sweat was starting to pool on my forehead. Being a balance is one thing but helping these demons bring fear and destruction to the world was not right. "Do you really think there isn't a balance still unchecked for that? Do you believe that they have needed my help in a very long time? When was the last time you watched the news and thought the world seems pretty happy today? The Demons know the limits and test them frequently to see if I am paying attention. I do what I can but there are many balances that still remain unmarked."

  He was right of course, when wasn't he, it didn't make all those deaths go away. Did he really see human life as a check mark on a sheet somewhere? "Why are you helping me? Why not stay out of it? Why not stay in some Buddhist temple somewhere you would be appreciated?" Saying this made him laugh harder than I had heard him laugh yet. "Cheryl, you are the balance to the evil they have visited on the world. You have a great many gifts to give this world that even you aren't aware of yet. I can only offer the equal to what you feel, to what was lost." he said and waved his hand toward my staff, a spiral spun down from the top to the bottom glowing for a second and then it was gone. I looked back at the road and back at him and he was gone. Crap, he never answered me again. What had he done to my staff. I reached out and touched it. I couldn't feel anything different. It felt just like it always had, polished wood with a smaller end on one side and a flat end on the other to hold onto.

I saw the city lights after my ears popped for the hundredth time, Now I was officially in the mile high city, it was all downhill from here. I reached out and found a source of light in a small hotel that was more my style, few people, cash only, no questions. I set up my new hammock to avoid sleeping in an all you can eat buffet for bed bugs. I reached out again. Nothing, the whole night and day thing was getting screwed up. The daylight started to break as I passed out. Just blackness behind my eyelids even with the cheap curtains here.

CHAPTER THIRTY-FIVE

I could see a giant mound in front of me and millions of ancient looking people surrounding it. I looked closer; they were averting their eyes, looking down in deep bows on their knees. Paint adorned most of them and animal skin for clothes. I looked up at the mound. It was impossibly high, but at the top there was a single man. I knew him, it was Father Ryan. He cast his eyes about not seeing me and pointed. Each woman or small child he pointed at were swept from the crowd by his Scions and carried to the top. They climbed and scrambled while some of their captives struggled. Other captives lay perfectly still as they were carried. The crowd didn't move at all, even the ones closest to the taken didn't twitch. After a dozen or so were swept up the side they all vanished. The crowd stood as they walked through me and near me I could see some with tears on their faces. I wondered if they could have fought back even if they wanted to. One inconsolable woman was being carried. They didn't speak English but I got the impression that her whole family had been claimed like this. They filed for an eternity past me in numbers I didn't dare to count. I knew somehow they would be back for next year's offering.

I woke up sweating, there was fresh snow outside and the heater in my room was really crap at keeping up, but I was covered in sweat like I was back in the sauna. I was clutching my staff. Two thoughts occurred to me, These sacrifices were just as fresh in my memory as the people I had seen slaughtered that night, and I suddenly knew the forth reason the Scions had burned my cottage in Sequoia. They had to get the Bible out of my hands. There was something in there that they didn't want me finding. Four o'clock in the afternoon, I went hunting for a similar Bible.

CHAPTER THIRTY-SIX

I learned two things in Denver, it is huge, and even being in the best shape of my life hadn't prepared me for this. I searched old book shops for hours. It turns out that most of Denver followed the New York state of mind, never sleeping. The bookstores were incredibly helpful but as it turns out there is more than one Bible, who knew. They all seem pretty close to each other but when I said this out loud I am pretty sure a woman with a cross on her neck actually hissed at me. None of them were like the one I had been reading. NIV, King James, etc... They all seemed like they were small in comparison to the larger tome I had been lugging across the country for a year. After the third store clerk to click her tongue at me I was done with these religious stores. I didn't see the little occult bookstore until I was on the other side of the street.

I walked in and the huge poster of Chakra points and useful crystals put me off. I nearly turned and left then. "Hi, you look very lost. So lost you are where you need to be." The woman speaking was tiny. She might be five foot tall if that, Blonde hair cut in a short style I could never pull off. She had big green eyes and they were wide. Like cartoon wide. "I was about to close up but something about your aura say's I should help you." I swear I tried not to roll my eyes at the word aura. I'm just bad at executing. "Hi, I'm Sara." I was slightly hesitant to shake her hand. I don't know why. Call it prejudice, call it disbelief, call it whatever you want. People that went around talking about this stuff were loonies.

I couldn't be rude though. I stuck my hand out to shake hers and she grabbed my wrist and turned my palm face up. I felt an electrical charge run from every place her skin touched mine. It felt like a buzz when it reached my head. I thought there was something wrong. I was ready to hit her, and then I realized she was one of those palm people on top of the other stuff. She didn't say anything. She just let my wrist go and stepped a little back. She gave me another once over with her eye's it was different; they stayed unfocussed like that priest in Atlanta. She actually made a gasping sound. I thought people only did that in cheesy movies or equally cheesy books. "How can I help you" Her voice dropped an octave. It was enough of a change I looked around for a second to find the source. "I need a Bible, but not one of those tiny little ones the religious store sells." I said. "Is it in English?" She was the second person to ask me that. I could read it. "Yeah, it would have to be." "Well we need to look down this aisle. I noticed as she led me, she never took her eyes off me. She even smiled a little. "If it is a bigger Bible you are looking for I suggest you start here." She pointed at a huge row of old books. None of them looked right but maybe the inside was what mattered.

I tried to look in peace, Sara made sure that didn't happen. She stayed within three feet of me since she started leading me to the books. "You must be exhausted." I thought about it, nothing about me said tired, no bags under my eyes, I didn't slump, nothing at all to give her that impression. "Why do you say that?" "You've only been finding yourself for a year now. Most people take their whole lives for that journey and in small pieces. You went into it with everything and never stopped." Whoa, I felt out and didn't feel anything really abnormal but she smiled when I did it. Some small points of light and a few of dark. Nothing at all from her direction though.

I reached out a hand and pushed on her shoulder. I wanted to see if she was real. She did some crazy spin and dropped her hips to the ground. She took my arm with her. I was used to being the woman to get the upper hand. I reversed the lock with a spin of my own grabbing her thumb as I went. I didn't even finish locking her arm before she squeezed her thumb back into position and spun me to the ground on my back. Jesus, was she the world thumb wresting champion, I dropped three hundred pound men with that move. "What does a Sprite want with my store and my books?" she looked at me not letting up. A fight wasn't going to get me anywhere. She called me a Sprite. But she was human. None of this made sense. I thought about lying to her. Did that make me better than the double-speaking demons or evasive ArchAngels?

"I am hunting a demon, I can't say his name but he is bad news and not afraid to kill regular mortals to make a point." "You have always been a Sprite but turned it aside for this long, why?" "My mom was a scientist, I was a scientist, if you know I am a Sprite then you also know the deal with my father." The pressure lightened a little but didn't stop entirely. "So you chose to not believe in yourself?" I never thought of it like that. "I didn't believe in my heaven or hell, or any other." "What started you on your path?" she let up with the pressure completely but left me lying on the ground. She pulled me up slowly; I made sure to keep my hands back and neutral. I didn't want her to think I was attacking again; she obviously had the mortal prowess to seriously hurt me. "Some of this particular Demon's Scions jumped me at my birthday party." "That was a year ago huh?" I nodded, more to get the crick out of my neck. She was strong for such a tiny person.

"He decided to make his point in many ways, but yeah it is was a year ago." "It" she said in response. I shook my head a little waiting for more of a sentence than just It "It, what?" I asked. "Demons and Angels are it's not he's or she's" I cocked my head like a puppy not understanding something. "Humans create the idea of him and her. Demon's and Angels are much older. If you see one as a male or female it is because you want to."

I liked Sara, not just because she could kick my butt. She talked in English. When I asked a question she answered. We both combed through her books to find the Bible I needed. I tried to explain it but I didn't do a good job of it. I told her it was big. That didn't quite mean the same thing to me that it did to her. Her books were much older but not as old as the one that I had with me for almost a year. "You know most of these are banned versions." "They ban Bible's? I thought they just did that to the books about magic and anything else that didn't mesh with religious dogma."

"There are plenty of Bibles that don't mesh with the current church beliefs" she said. I never thought about people banning a Bible. Did they burn them like some of the churches did to other books and cd's back home? "How did you know what I was?" I asked in the most casual way I could muster. "How did you know I was Human?" I thought about it for a minute. "I felt out for anything dark, only a few pinpricks here and there, nothing big enough to be a Scion or Demon." "That is similar to how I do it. Plus your palm and aura are practically screaming at me." "What's an aura look like?" She looked at me as if I asked her what the sun looked like. "It isn't

just a glow from a person, sometimes it looks like
a stain or burn. Every being is different." She
didn't seem to be all there. Like halfway through
the sentence she drifted off. I waited a second for
her eye's to focus again. "Sorry, mini seizure."
she said. "I thought those made people fall out,
shake and swallow their tongue." She laughed
for the first time. It was a sweet laugh that fit
with her voice when I first met her. "Are you O.K.
now?" I asked. "It was a minor one. I will live for
a while yet." I didn't know to take this. Was it a
joke or did she really know when she would die. I
had never met anyone like her back home. They
would have chased her out of town with stones
and pitchforks. She giggled. "Sorry, the idea of
me being chased out of a small town is funny; I
technically was when I was little." Holy crap, she
read my thoughts. "Only flashes hun no worries,
all your secrets are safe with me, it is mostly
pictures anyway." she said and turned back to the
book aisles. I could see a devilish smile that made
me wonder what she saw.

After another half hour I thought about it. If
she could see some images, maybe she could
help me find the Bible easier if she saw what it
looked like. I told her what I was going to try.
She seemed to like the idea. I tried to picture it
as perfectly as I could. The feeling of the paper,
the oversized lettering, the flowing handwriting
instead of typed print. I didn't expect the look of

shock on her face when I finished. "You said it was in English." "Well yeah, I don't speak any other languages except a few words of Spanish and read even fewer." "Do you know what Coptic is? "Umm, I don't think I ever heard that word before. Does that matter?" I asked. "It matters quite a bit actually. You said it was big, how big?" I tried to gesture with my hands but she shook her head. I don't know of any complete Bible that big, even in Coptic. Did it include a chapter from Thomas?" I tried to think about the list at the front. "Yeah, and someone named Judas and another named Solomon, is that important." "It isn't just important, it is impossible. Those weren't discovered until recently. It hasn't been a part of the Bible, ever." "It existed; it was old enough to fit in a museum somewhere. I didn't imagine it for a years' worth of reading." That was the first thing that made her blink. I thought she was going to have another seizure, then she threw a hand in the air. "Got it" she said. "Why don't we create the Bible for you from the Apocrypha and several other non-canon Bibles and build something similar?" There was a bubbly side to her voice I never heard before. She was really excited by this challenge. Maybe if I knew when and how I would die, I would find excitement in just breathing. It took less than twenty minutes but she seemed like a blur going section to section like that. When she was done she had an impressive stack of books.

I tried to figure out how to carry them but she produced a cloth bag and tied it to my staff. I hope I didn't get jumped on my way back to the hotel. Feeling the weight of them on the staff, I hoped I did get jumped. The mass alone would send them flying. "Thanks for everything Sara." She looked at me with that long off look. "Oh I will see a lot of you I am sure." The door rang when I opened it. When did it get so dark out? I did my best to hurry back trying to not think about the implications of Sara's words. I didn't stop to ask myself why Belial had been the one to give the original Bible to me either. I think I know why it was wrapped in paper though. I don't think he could have touched it himself.

I plopped the haul down on my bed. There was one odd book in the bunch. If it wasn't so dog-eared, It might have been something she gave everyone. "Theories and Practical Meditation" was scrawled across the cover. Did I make my first real friend without having to lie to them since this started? Sara made me comfortable, anyone that could take me in a straight up fight like that was impressive, the fact that she was only five foot tall said even more about her ability. She really was everything I wasn't. I was always thinking, she was feeling. I needed to make sure if I survived this trip to come back to see her again. She knew things and would actually tell me.

CHAPTER THIRTY-SEVEN

In two days, and two different locations, what were the odds of running across people I met elsewhere? I hoped for the best. I knew it wouldn't be true, but I had to try. "Maureen." I yelled as I saw her a few steps in front of me. She turned around and the vagueness in her eyes was missing. They looked sharp and clear. "Hello Cheryl, what are you doing here of all places?" she asked. Maybe she came up here to get her eye's fixed. Maybe there was some other excuse. Maybe I was the pope too. Any of those things could have been true. I just knew none of them were. We got closer, "When did he give you your sight back?" She looked away for a second blushing. "The Father prayed over me and I woke up like this. I realized I only stayed in that little town because I was scared of seeing anything new. Now that I can see, I have so many places I want to witness for myself." It was the old Maureen, Did she really become healed? If anyone had earned it through faith it was her.

"What about your crush?" I should have been embarrassed to ask, but I had a feeling there was a story behind her change of heart. "You weren't there Monday morning were you?" she asked. I didn't say anything and just shook my head. I didn't want to stop her from talking if I could help it. "Jeremiah announced his engagement to one of the Johnson girls. I wouldn't call it an arranged marriage, but the church got a much needed upgrade right after the announcement. I think they wanted Cassie to be remembered as the preacher's wife, instead of the car stealing, drug dealing eighteen year old we all knew." "I'm sorry." I'm not sure why I said it but it felt right. "Don't be, you could say that opened my eyes figuratively and literally." Maureen said.

"I almost gave this up", she produced the plastic coin she had the entire time I knew her. Then the best thing in the world happened and I was given the ability to see again and didn't feel like having that drink after all. It was a fresh start for me." I wanted to ask her what it cost her, but I knew from experience she might not know. It could also be divine intervention. I really had no idea. "I always wanted to see the north and the mountains. Now I get to, I have nothing holding me back." Now that I looked at her she looked younger too. I could see the explorer Maureen that was hiding underneath this whole time. "What's next for you now?" I asked. This was the first time I had seen any evidence of something good happening for someone that deserved it. "I will probably keep heading north until they ask for my passport then head east." "That sounds perfect." "What about you Cheryl? Where are you headed? I wanted to tell her but something pulled at my thoughts in the last second before they reached my mouth. "A little further north, then after that who knows." I am letting the wind decide after that." She knew I wasn't from this area, even though we never talked about where I was from. "Well I hope you find everything you need like I have. It is really freeing to be able to just pack up and go when you need to, but it is just as good to find where you belong." I don't know why I felt like that was the end of the conversation. For some reason we both just said "Bye" at the same time. Maureen with a spring in her step took off up the street. Knowing at least one good thing happened this year probably put a spring in my step too. I forgot about the food I was searching for and headed back to the hotel.

I knew it was the middle of the night but I wasn't tired. The altitude alone had given me a workout. So what was there to do for a demon slaying, no job having, woman in a strange town? I turned on the TV and crashed in my hammock. My favorite episode of Buffy was on, I sang to each number, laughed at some of the sillier bits, and did the usual aw when the final song brought my dream characters together. After it was over I couldn't find anything else to watch so I just turned it off. A random thought made me laugh. I was the modern version of the stuff I grew up on, but my day to day life was too boring to ever make a TV show or story out of. They never showed characters so bored they did another set of chin ups because it had been months since anything at all had happened while hiding in a forest all alone. My car was definitely a cuter way to get where I needed to be than any of my fictional character heroines. If I thought about this too long it would point back to my fear that I was crazy, and I was living out the life of my TV show upbringing. Somewhere in all of this, I fell asleep, still comparing a TV show to my real life.

I had another dream of people being slaughtered to Father Ryan's delight. They were high on a pyramid shaped structure made of earth, lined up like cattle waiting for their chance to die. Tens of thousands were gathered in the area around it watching but not in horror but excitement. As a body would fly down trailing blood from the top of the pyramid, the others would attack the body. After one of the most gruesome things I had ever seen, each one of the attackers started sprouting black sinew from their arms and back until they were completely covered. The newly minted Scions would then take another set of stairs to stand beside Father Ryan. Dear God.

I woke up covered in sweat and once again felt out for anything around. Just a few people, people were a good thing. That meant there wasn't an all-out assault coming. The humans would have been killed to keep me from hearing anything that might tip me off. I realized what all of these dreams had in common, the timing and where I needed to be. A platform, a ritual, the making of Scions. Belial wasn't just randomly choosing places. He needed an audience, he needed sacrifices. That also explained Amon mentioning the demons that collected people's souls, I needed to put a stop to it, at least the one I could control. After all these years the numbers in Belial's armies had to be huge and the more they grew the more likely he could do everything he was planning. That is why Amon didn't try to stop me, he knew the future, he knew about this power play. That also meant I was going to win somehow, if he could see me losing, he wouldn't have placed his bets on letting such a prize go. Despite his disregard for Demons all being the same, I bet he collected something like souls or he wouldn't have his own Scions. I got all of my stuff together and dropped off the room keys in the night slot. I tore out of the parking lot and headed straight to the nearest platform, the aptly named Devils Tower. GPS said it was a six hour drive, wonder if I could prove it wrong.

CHAPTER THIRTY-EIGHT

I didn't even make it to the border of Denver. A car was parked sideways across the road with smoke billowing from the hood. In front of the car, a man stood waving his arms. He was short with glasses and was shivering from the cold. His bald head gleaming in the moonlight. Why didn't he have a hat or something to keep his body heat in? He couldn't look more helpless if he had pink fuzzy ears. I didn't realize how short he was until I got out of the car to see if I could help. I used to be pretty good with cars. This car was older than me, it would be pretty simple to fix. That beat trying to get it off the road. "Thank you, can you help me get this stupid thing to the side of the road?" he just guessed I was there to push that behemoth. I might be tall and strong but I wasn't going to push something I could fix and drive off the road.

"Let me take a look and I might be able to get you back on the road." The little man twitched, I guess he never thought of a woman being able to fix a car. He was still standing in the same place. I vaguely wondered if there was some super strength glue holding his feet to the ground. I walked around the car and stuck my head under the hood. It was a really old Chevy. I liked working on them. Everything was spaced apart enough to reach in and fix any piece. I could probably just tighten the oil cap. The smoke coming from the engine smelled like oil. I looked down and saw nothing obviously wrong except the smoke coming from the fresh oil on the exhaust. There was nothing wrong with.

I didn't get to finish the thought. The hood slammed down on my head. The next few minutes were a daze. I was bleeding, my head was spinning, but there were no Scions anywhere near. Somewhere, a thousand miles away, I heard some scuffling noises and then something gasping for breath. It wasn't me gasping. My head didn't clear until a tiny blond figure stepped up beside me. I might have to fight like this. That would seriously suck. The voice was soft and rhythmic. "Sprite, you will be OK. This should help some." I smelled something strong. The world spun one more time and then came into focus. Sara was kneeling over me with a smile that stretched from dimple to dimple. She was dabbing something wet on my head and I was reminded of the old priest in Georgia, except she did have something in her hand. I never smelled anything like the stuff she was putting on my cuts, but it worked great. The ringing in my ears was gone and I didn't even have a headache from the attack.

I looked over and saw the little man laying on the ground, He was breathing but his eyes were closed. "Is he going to be OK?" I asked. Sara blinked for a second. She seemed a little confused herself. "Oh, you can't see it can you?" "Can't see what?" I asked. "His aura." I felt really dumb being the only person not putting this together. "Why would little man attack me?" "That isn't a man, or at least not what I would call a man. He's a thrall." she said. "What's a thrall?" I asked. "A thrall used to be a human until they accepted a deal with a demon. Then they become a kind of slave. They can go on living their life for years until the Demon collects and forces them to do something specific." "So you're saying this guy is what, a pre-Scion." Sara scratched at her nose absently. It was cute."Yeah, that is close enough." "Why can't I feel him like I can the Scion's then?" "Because, he hasn't gone fully over. His aura is dark and stained but it isn't completely black. I can teach you to see the aura's but it will take longer than you have right now."

That snapped something in my head. "How did you know I was going to need some help? I have been fighting my way across the country for a year now." She took my hand and flipped it over as she pulled me up to sit. The minute her hand touched mine, I felt that electric charge run through me again. Touching her was like playing with a Van De Graaff generator. "You have a few more trials but I think they are only meant to slow you down. This attack was more of a hail mary pass." "You can see all that in my palm?" I asked. "No, but I can get a sense of what is ahead when I touch you." She blushed a little. I guess she realized how that sounded after she said it.

"Thank you, if he, or it, is trying to slow me down I better get moving. I know you are seriously amazing in a fight" I nodded at the still prone man on the ground. "These things aren't the same as people though." I said. "I know." she said. She sounded sad. Maybe she really wanted to be able to fight them. I put my loose hand on her back and I stood up. I was trying to be reassuring. I didn't expect her to start crying.

"What's wrong?" I tried to think of anything I may have said or done. Nothing. "Just another flash. Stay safe Sprite, we really want you to stay around for a while." That was the oddest thing anyone ever said to me. The "we" part and the "stay around" part too. She was alone, as far as I knew, and I haven't stayed anywhere for long. I couldn't grasp at what she said, so I stuck with a basic reassurance. "I am tougher than I look, I'm not going anywhere for a while. I will come back to see you next week.

CHAPTER THIRTY-NINE

I thought about everything Sara told me so far. It really was like living in another world. I just met her but she acted as if we were best friends since we were kids. Some part of my brain broke at this point. I just couldn't think about it anymore. I needed a distraction. It was too dark for any real sight seeing while I drove. My ears were popping regularly but other than that, nothing at all happened.

I really should stop throwing the bored vibe around. I didn't make it more than a few miles before the engine sputtered on my car. She couldn't break on me now. We've both been through too much not to finish this properly. Then a crunching sound put an end to the sounds from the motor. Just as my precious Mini was coasting to the side of the road I caught sight of what I was expecting. I just didn't think they grew that large. A white hair Scion was charging at my car from the side. He was the size of a large bull. If he hit me I would be climbing through glass and wrecked metal to fight him.

I was only seconds from impact, then it felt warm in the car. Juan was sitting there smiling at me from the passenger seat. He never said a word. Then he vanished, and so did my car. I was standing on an old highway with my staff. I had a quarter of a second to react to the new setting. The Scion came in and swung for me with one long clawed hand. It missed but barely. I missed my attack on him by a mile. I knew he would already be circling around for another attack. I reached out to feel for the rest of them. It was just him, maybe the cold was getting to me. I swung up and across when he came closer. I caught his arm but he didn't burst into flames so easily. Maybe his size had something to do with it. Wouldn't a big candle still burn as easy as a little one?

I jumped and rolled forward over his other arm as he tried another swing. The big brute wanted to go toe-to-toe with me. I could take that. I spun and struck at him over and over but each strike was less effective than they usually were with this type of Scion. I needed a game changer before he landed a hit of his own. He was much faster than anything his size had a right to be. I missed one swing by less than an inch. I wasn't interested in a haircut. I really wasn't interested in one that started at my shoulders. I turned the staff and smashed it down on the ground and tried to fry him like I did with the ones that attacked me inside my car. If I couldn't set him on fire I could take him out with a lightning bolt.

I struck down and felt the energy pouring out of me. The fire snake flew straight toward him, but the moment it nearly touched him he jumped. The fire snake traveled harmlessly off into the distance. I couldn't hit him like that if he wasn't touching the ground. That would have been good information a long time ago. I knew I couldn't do anything but dive out of the way. The pavement was going to hurt but the relative pain of road rash versus being eviscerated seemed a better alternative. I had just enough time to turn onto my back as he dove on top of me. I thrust the staff out and pushed as much energy through it as I could. When it broke the hide of sinew he rebounded like I hit him with a car. Like the spiky Scions he burned from the inside out. I didn't even watch as he burned. I knew there wouldn't be much left of him in a few seconds. Something else caught my eye though. My Mini sitting exactly where it was before with Juan leaning against the nose of the car.

"That was well done. What is that saying about being able to adapt and winning?" he said. He knew the precise words to the quote, he was doing his best to not show off. "Where did you go and what did you do to my baby?" He blinked back at me. It was dark, but I could make out every part of his face, even from a bit of a distance. "I knew none of your side were going to help and I couldn't just watch as the Scion shredded your car. I took it to a friend in Fresno to fix it." I know the part of that statement I should have been curious about, instead my brain locked onto "You have friends, and they live in Fresno?" That made him laugh. "Yes Cheryl, I would say I have many friends around the world. Do you think you are the only important person on the planet?" Ouch. I knew he was tracking me most of the time but I never thought to ask what he did other than showing up at the right time to help me. I was tempted to ask what he was doing that whole time I was in Sequoia. I decided a change of subject was a little less squirmy feeling. "What did your friend do to my baby?" "You had a bad head-gasket, Manny went ahead and rebuilt the motor." I wanted to do that sideways look of confusion, I just had a feeling that if I asked anything else I would feel silly for not realizing myself. I'm sure people rebuild engines in a matter of minutes all the time. "Is there anything else?" I was ready to get back on the road. I could feel the clock ticking down in my head. I did my best to make it clear I was leaving regardless of what he said. I walked over to my car and opened the door. The blingy gearshift was still there. I was worried that little piece would be gone for some reason. Juan just watched as I packed my staff back into the car. He was seriously cute, but I had a date with a Demon. "I will make sure you are not disturbed further Cheryl. You have a full plate ahead of you. Good Luck." He was gone before the end of the word luck was finished. I felt very alone. I was standing on the side of a highway with my car, It would only be a short time before I was either destroying a demon or dying. I don't think there was a middle ground.

CHAPTER FORTY

I made it in good time after that. It was still dark out and everything was peaceful. Too peaceful, there should be something happening here. The huge tower in front of me shadowed and empty of people. Maybe the Scions were in hiding. I couldn't feel them but I felt a huge amount of power. The power didn't have the feathery feel of good or the oily feel of evil. It was just power. I kept hearing my mom's voice "calm before the storm." She used to say that anytime I complained about being bored. I knew I was going to need some sleep for tonight. If I come back here at midnight I might get the jump on him or it or whatever. I still couldn't get that part straight.

I stopped at an RV campsite that would let me just crash for the same price as one of those big houses on wheels. But they had showers, and proper restrooms. After getting clean I ate and slept a perfectly dreamless sleep with warmth all around me.

I woke up to the hectic atmosphere of the tourists. All of them had to be somewhere and in a hurry. They acted like this was the last time anyone would see this place. "For some of them that might be true." a little voice in my head whispered. I thought about all the things that kept me going. I couldn't name one. Juan wasn't who he said he was, my mom thought I was still around, no one knew I was gone. They wouldn't even know if I died here today. Why did I even care? Then the little boys face popped in my head. He was why I did this. Him and all the others that never did anything but stand too close to me. I wondered if the people here were in danger just because I was nearby.

No, they were in danger whether I was here or not. Belial would be here. I owed him something. I had the phone for a year now. I never made a single call on it before today. Was it something telling that the first person I called was Sara? She switched tones so fast it made my head spin. "Hello, Thank you for calling... What's wrong?" How did she know it was me? Oh yeah Psychic, I forgot. "I don't know if I can do this, there are so many innocent people here." There was a shake in my voice, when did I become the girl with the shaky voice. "Did you practice the stuff from the other book I gave you?" "Not really, I looked at it. Then all these people started walking by." "You realize every person there was called. They have all made some kind of deal with the demon even if they don't know it." She paused for a second. I was about to check to make sure we were still connected. "Just practice what I sent you and I will see you in a few days." She was so certain, I was too. I knew I would see her again soon. I just hoped it wasn't due to me running again. "OK, what do I do if I run into the balance guy again?" I was careful not to use his familiar name. I didn't even want to think about him right now. "You'll know what to do." She sounded sad about that part. "I'll go do what the book says. If nothing else it will help lower my blood pressure." "There you go Sprite, you can do what you want but the world is funny about driving you to do the right thing." That was it. No goodbye, nothing. She hung up. I was beginning to think I was the only person left in my life to say goodbye before leaving.

I found my hands were still shaking as I held the phone. I kept looking at the screen long after it had gone to sleep. Reflected in the screen were just a set of eye's. Now they were crying. I pressed the wake button and began dialing. I nearly hung up after each ring. After the third ring I heard the familiar "Hello?" I wanted to tell her everything. I wanted to cry so hard that she could hold me through the phone. I also knew she would be the first to stand me upright and tell me to work through my problems. "Hi mom. I don't have much time but wanted to call and tell you that I love you." There was a bit of silence. "I love you too sweetie. You can tell me all about your day when you come over tonight. Oh, and don't forget the ice cream this time." I wanted to cry again but for different reasons. As much as I was missing her and even my sometimes lame co-workers, they didn't miss me. I knew it was to insulate them but it isolated me. It was merciful in the way a beheading is merciful. You still have the pieces to bury but the person isn't really there. I wanted to say more. It had been a year of constant fear and panic. A year of winning and losing. Somehow none of that mattered right now. Right now it was a conversation with the only person I loved and they just saw me yesterday. A year of yesterday's I wouldn't get back. "Well they need that expense report, I have to go." "OK sweetie, will you be bringing that nice kid Juan over tonight?" My brain started reeling. Mom never met Juan. Whatever they did to her was so complete it came as a package deal, boyfriend and all. "I think so; I will have to ask if he can." "Well you take care and be safe, lots of loonies out tonight. Love ya, bye." "I'll be careful." and I hung up. The irony that I didn't say goodbye before hanging up wasn't lost on me. I wanted to have a total meltdown. There was too much to process. I only had hours until I had to be focused. I sat and wiped a few errant tears from the pages of Sara's book as I read it. It kept talking about finding balance, what I needed had nothing to do with balance and everything to do with justice. I wanted my life back, I wanted my boring job back, I wanted my bland co-workers back. I knew none of that was coming back unless I found a way to push it all in a hole until after the fight.

I found a suitable place to practice meditating. I only had a few sneers as I sat in the middle of the grass and closed my eyes and tried to control my breathing. I sat there for what seemed hours, or minutes, I couldn't tell. When I opened my eye's Juan was there. Only we weren't sitting in a field near Devils Tower. "You're ready to do what is needed?" he asked. Where was this magical mind reading fairy dust and where could I get some of it. "I think so, who do I need?" I asked him out loud. Only one of us reading minds was one too many, or one too few. "You already know, you just have to find out the price."

CHAPTER FORTY-ONE

I wasn't prepared for what I saw when I got to the Devil's Tower. The area was supposed to be empty except for rangers patrolling to keep people out at night. It was packed. No one even noticed the Scions packed into the crowds of regular humans. I saw a male body shoved off the side of the huge rock to free fall into an inevitable crash at the bottom. Several in the crowd attacked the remains like already feral animals just like in my dream. They all began transforming like the dream as well, sinew wrapping their skin. I wondered if like the first ones I saw, did they all still look human to the spectators. I had grown so use to looking past their fake image, I had forgotten about the mask they wore in public.

The crowd was dressed in all manner of clothes, some in night clothes too light for this climate but not shivering from the cold. Tourists, they were almost all tourists. All of them with a blank look in their eyes. Like a book had opened in my head I could picture the word enthrall in the old Bible. They weren't here willingly, and the new Scions didn't do that of their own accord. I doubted they even knew what they were signing up to do. That was what Juan, the ArchAngels, Sara, even Amon had been trying to tell me. He was cheating, he was enthralling people with lies. Free will was being negated. The ArchAngels were powerless to stop him because of long forgotten rules, but I sure as hell wasn't. I could do whatever I wanted. What I wanted was to find a way up there. I wasn't much of a climber and pretty sure I would get cut down as soon as I tried it. I stood behind the crowd as far from the Scions as I could. I needed a plan. I needed to just shoot my way to the top. I wasn't a demon I couldn't just jump up there.

I went around the outside of the crowd until it thinned. I didn't see a light source but could see Father Ryan clearly still. It must be some kind of demon thing. I could see somewhere fairly clear with a straight shot to the top. Even in the less packed area there were still throngs of people and Scions all standing around. First I tried just calmly walking up to the side. That worked for about ten steps. I bumped into a chubby man but the moment I touched him the black sinew strands came bursting from his back and wrapping around him. Before I had time to blink, he was a full Scion and already reaching for me. I dodged out of the way but ran into a frail looking lady. The same thing happened to her. Was everyone here already a Scion just waiting to be turned on somehow? I realized even the thinner crowd now looked like an impossible maze of death. They stood too close for me to get through without touching them and the old woman was now an agile female Scion. I batted her claws down with my staff and thrust the other end into the shoulder of the newly created male to my right. More started coming my way, I noticed the human looking ones were still staring up at Father Ryan with blank expressions.

I might be able to use their malaise to my advantage. I blew the new male Scion back through the crowd. He didn't even register with the people he bowled over. They just got back up and continued staring at the top of the tower. I came up with a plan to get to the face of the tower without touching too many of them The other Scion came at me from behind, I couldn't remember her passing me but they didn't seem to be communicating as a group. That would work in my favor. Then just as she tried to rip my spine out I rolled forward into the only clear area around. I understood now. She was the mate to the one I blew across the crowd. They would always be connected. I didn't want to cause anymore Scions to come sprouting out of the crowd but I didn't need to waste time or energy on this one either. Telling myself none of these people were completely human helped even if it was probably wrong. I could figure that out later. Right now, I waited until the female was in mid-leap and blew a small fireball straight into her head. That was the humane thing to do right? The hulking mass of the male was behind me again but that was where I wanted him. I blasted him back through the crowd into the rock face creating a path for me to take. I didn't see any other male or female Scions, and as long as I didn't bump anyone I wouldn't create more. Maybe the ones down here still had a chance if I took out Belial before they were turned.

CHAPTER FORTY-TWO

I got right up near the rock tower and pointed my staff at the ground. I prayed this worked the way I planned it. I shot force straight down at the ground beneath me, like when I blasted the Scions. Instead of launching something away from me I used it like a rocket. I shot myself straight up the side. I nearly overshot it. Guess I was rested up. There were only a small handful of Scions up here, but I had a feeling when they knew I was here it would be very different. I could feel their inky blackness under each one standing with their back to me. I followed the plan and took them all out at once like I had at the hotel. I gathered up the power and drove it into the rock at my feet. "Oh Belial." I yelled as beams of blue-white fire shot like a spotlight straight out of the ground at all of their feet. They didn't just disintegrate, they were gone completely, no ash nothing, erased.

Father Ryan didn't even flinch. He continued mutilating the poor overweight man in the multicolor shorts and threw him down the side. Then said in his most polite voice "I am glad to see you made it, Angel." He had to know why I was here. "You won't be so glad in a minute." I replied in the grittiest voice I could manage. "Did you think I wasn't planning all along to get you here? This is my seat, my throne now. Amon cannot take it back and when I sacrifice you. You will fuel an army of the strongest Scions Hell has ever known.

We will be more prepared than Amon could have ever made us. I prepared another burst instead of letting him monologue. I struck the ground with my staff and put a ton of energy into it. I saw lights all over the ground below me as Scions in the crowd burst and became nothing like the ones up here had. I realized too late I couldn't feel an inky stain under Father Ryan anymore. It was like he was above the ground just barely. He was only an inch off the ground but he wasn't touching it.

 "Do you think I would let myself be caught by such a pretty parlor trick? The Scions are disposable; I have been gathering them for eons. Speaking of gathering, I think you know my friend here." I didn't want to look. I knew before I saw her. I knew the moment she appeared in Denver with her eyesight restored. The politics of religion drove this wonderful woman into the worst parts of despair. I looked into Maureen's eyes one more time. Her lip quivered just a little and I swore she even began apologizing but the bands of black sinew covered her so fast it may have just been wishful thinking. I didn't want to hurt her, she was my friend. One of my only friends that didn't ask me for anything in return. Now I knew just how much she suffered. How much each of the beings I killed so easily suffered. What else could I do? The helplessness must have been part of Belial's plan. My left arm and left leg paid the price. Bloody gashes appeared on both

as not-Maureen the Scion ran by and slashed
at me. She could have sliced me into pieces but
she only left flesh wounds. Some part of her was
holding back. I knew I had to destroy her and I
knew that whatever might be left of her wanted
me to. She was just another Scion. She was also
one of the few human connections I had in my
new life. I blasted her back with wind but held
back on the fire. I couldn't, on her next charge
I had to. I jumped out of the way but instead of
punching her with my fire covered hand, I ran
my hand across her cheek. I knew it wouldn't
matter but it did to me. It was just as I landed that
I remembered the core structure of the Scions I
neglected. For every female, there was a male.
I saw Father Richardson change and hit me just
below the hips in a split-second. He drove me six
feet backwards and I skidded to a halt with him
on top of me. If Belial thought I felt the same way
about Father Richardson he was dead wrong. I
grabbed for his leg but missed. He put each clawed
hand on my legs. That was his play; it was a good
one too. I couldn't freeze up now, I had to fight
back, I had to do something, I wasn't helpless. I
only froze for an instant. The memory still hot
in my head but getting the sickening black claws
off my legs before he could maim me was a much
bigger thought. I grabbed both hands before he
could sink his claws in and pushed enough fire
through them to melt a bus. He turned to ash

without a single breath between my thought and his ignition. I beat both of his trump cards. Why didn't I feel like I was winning?

I felt a crushing weight of darkness as hundreds of Scions appeared on the top of the tower. It felt like they were sitting on my chest and I couldn't take in a breath without sucking in some of their putrid evil. I had never dealt with them like this before. I looked for Father Ryan, he was walking toward me but the closer he got, the more I could see a gaunt demon with white hair on top of his head, the scars I had seen on Father Ryan's flesh in the Sauna mirrored on the demon's flesh. Something had hurt him before, If I just had some idea what that was it would be great. When he got close enough he swung out with a clawed blackened hand. It struck my upraised staff and stopped. I was surprised because I expected him to cut it like a toothpick; he seemed to have the same thought. He used his other hand to knock me off balance as all of his Scions looked as though they were frothing at the mouth to attack me. They were here as spectators. He needed spectators. Every time he had built power in my dreams he had huge masses of people that were neither there to be sacrificed or to become Scions. He needed people to witness it, he needed their fear. That was what he was trying to hide from me in the old Bible. I parried his next swing with another block from my staff and tried a more direct fire punch.

He neatly caught my arm and spun it to the side with a sickening crack. Something broke, I didn't know how badly but the bone was still inside, that was a positive. The pain took a second to register. Just as the wave of nausea hit me, he swept my feet and pounced onto my hips holding me to the rock. I tried to focus another blast through my staff in my good right hand but I couldn't even point it at him from this angle with him on my hips pinning me with his claws. The pain was pulling the power from my strike nearly as fast as I could build it. Maybe Amon the seer of the future was wrong, Maybe Juan shouldn't have wasted so much time to change this to a check mark in his damned balance book. Belial was going to be too powerful to stop now. When he killed me he would have Scions that would be strong enough to be demons in their own right. "Why Me?" was all I could get out.

CHAPTER FORTY-THREE

"Who else?" came Juan's voice in my head. Who else, I had let myself be chased around like some pawn. Then I heard Juan's voice again. This time it wasn't in my head though. It sounded like he brought a PA system with him. "Go back home, Forget this." his voice wasn't just commanding, it was no questions asked drill instructor commanding. This stopped Belial in midstrike. He didn't let up on my hips though and held my center of gravity still so I couldn't get loose. All of the people who had gathered, all the tourists, rangers, and locals made their way back into the darkness. The crowds were thinning out. Unfortunately for those that didn't get out first were too easy to pick off by the Scions in the crowd. Several hapless people were killed, not out of some ritual or rite. They were being killed out of sheer dumb luck and frustration by the Scions.

Belial watched passively as the throngs exited or were killed outright. Neither of which seemed to make him happy. I looked at my now swelling left arm, it was definitely broken. I wanted to cradle it but it was pinned to the ground, causing more waves of pain to shoot sporadically whenever Belial changed his grip or weight on it. He turned his cold eyes to look straight behind me, "You are not free to act Balance, and I have broken none of the rules. Just following my nature." The voice was a mix of a snake like sound and a car sliding on gravel. I could feel the darkness of everything around me; It felt like my entire world was filled with inky globs of putrid evil. It fought to get inside me; it was like it was trying to find some secret passage into my body.

That is when it hit me; I was giving up my chance. "What chance?" something whispered in my ear. That would be the blackness; I guess if blackness had a voice it would be sweet and charming. No one let the charging rhino in the door willingly. I tried to focus. I couldn't blast him with my staff. I couldn't hit him with my left arm, pinned down and broken as it were. There was something I could do, but the blackness was trying to cloud my reasoning. It was getting in the way. It was blocking my emotional response. It wasn't blocking rational thought though. I don't think evil understands a human's rational thought process. It is too based on the individual; every person's rational thought process is different. That is when I had it. I knew what I needed to do, I didn't want to do it, the downside seriously sucked. I sucked in a breath and held it. Then when I let it out I yelled my battle cry "I liked this shirt you bastard" my entire body burst into blue-white flame. Belial was thrown from me like I had sucker punched him. He flew into the ranks of his Scions. He limped back out smoldering from everywhere he had been touching me. I sprung up with the cloudiness of the dark fading from my mind and settling my staff firmly on the ground, still flickering blue-white flames brighter than before. Belial's Scions took this as a great time to attack me. First mistake, I struck my staff down, they burst into little spotlights of their own. I felt like the more power I needed the more was there.

The rest of the Scions seemed to pull back, then Belial screamed "Kill her." they responded like a pack of dogs being let off their leads. Last mistake, I stamped my flaming foot to the top of Devils Tower, and all of the Scions on top of the tower turned into a dazzling array of white and blue bursts of light. Leaving just Belial up here. I gritted my teeth in anger and pain at him, I wanted him to know that I was the reason he was done, for good. Before I could call anything else up I felt the weight of thousands of dark slimy Scions appearing at the base of the Tower.

They had to be Belial's full army. There were so many, and now that I know how most of them came to be, I felt sick again. Poor people tricked into servitude forever. Belial grinned at me, if you can call a black sinew wrapped demon with white hair something capable of smiling. "Even you do not have the power to take them all out, if even one gets out from under my control it will ravage whole towns before you can find him. Imagine the deathhhhhh." he drew out the last word like it was the name of his long lost love. "Women, Men, Childrennnnnnnn. And it will be because of your choice, no retribution will clear your conscience of that today or ever Angel." Belial finished. Still with the mockery of a smile he stalked toward me with still smoking craters where he had touched me. If I finished him now, it was going to be insanity and I doubt I could take them all. They all stood facing the stone walls of the tower as if waiting orders. Just bobbing up and down with each breath they took. I squared myself with Belial, still conflicted as I felt the inky darkness start to creep up the sides of the tower. His options were for me to die and let the demons spare the local towns or destroy him and have an even higher body count in my nightmares for the rest of my life.

He struck at my left arm but the moment the flames and his flesh touched it began to sizzle and splatter. The greasy remains of his flesh splattered onto my skin and felt like boiling oil. He didn't just catch fire and burn away like the Scion's. Of course it wouldn't be that easy. He dove forward so fast I barely had a moment to blink. I tried to blow him backwards with a wall of wind but it didn't even have time to build to a light gust before he bowled me over. I kicked at his flabby stomach and felt the boiling splatters of his flesh on the sole of my foot. Direct contact was not going to work. If I kept it up we would both be burnt husks and I didn't just burn away my favorite shirt and any amount of decency to die like that. The kick did manage to dislodge him though. He skidded on all fours with his claws digging into the top of the tower spinning as he went until he was facing me again. I struck at the open air trying to anticipate his leap but he changed directions at the last second and I only managed a glancing blow with my staff. He didn't completely avoid the impact though and the combination of the staff and the fire caused him to tumble as his left arm hung loose. He sprung back up and even from this distance I could see the oozing of the sinew re-knitting itself. If he kept rebuilding like that I would never be able to wear him down enough. I needed a game changer. I needed something to completely destroy him with one blow. I needed to stay alive in the process.

He raked his good arm across his sharpened teeth then swung his arm at the open air. I didn't recognize the threat until it was nearly too late. Gobs of that acid saliva were flying directly at my face. I didn't have time to duck; I just wanted to get out of the range of that goop. Belial became smaller. No, I was further back from him. I could see the globs of spit flying towards me but at a much greater distance. If I let them get through they would hit my chest and stomach. I pushed a fireball with some wind to meet it before it could reach me. He laughed and did it again, this time I just reappeared to the right and avoided it altogether. It was exactly what he wanted me to do. In the moments I was focused on the spit and moving he dove toward where I was going. We collided but both of us bounced and sizzled where our bodies had touched. "Give up little Sprite, you will be put to good use don't worry your life will change so much for this world."

Then I felt something else. I grinned maniacally at Belial. I couldn't believe it but I knew something he didn't. He wouldn't be so smug. I tucked and rolled toward him to hit him with a punch, but he leapt over me like I was a crack in the sidewalk. I spun and he attacked this time. I wanted to be on the other side of him. I needed to be on the other side of him. Then I was on the other side of him. I twisted my right arm behind me and spun the staff to its pointed end like a jousters lance and skewered his back and pinned him to the ground. "You forgot something Belial, no matter what claim you think you have, this is Amon's seat. Do you think the Demon famous for knowing future events wouldn't know you were planning this for eons? Did you really think you could mess with a real freaking Sprite and win?" I said as the sounds of ripping and tearing muscle were all around the tower. You were also right about me killing you. I think I am in line behind someone else. I pulled out the staff and flames ignited where it had entered, it was burning a slow hole in his back and his body was convulsing as I walked away. "He's all yours Amon, Don't expect another gift from me." I said to the night air. Behind me I could hear Belial screaming and Amon laughing that crazy laugh of his.

CHAPTER FORTY-FOUR

I got back down kind of the same way I had come in, albeit with a squishier landing. I walked past what was left of Belial's Scions. Amon's Scions were much more efficient, I would have to file that away in case I ever had to fight them in earnest in the future. I got to where I had left my car and leaning against it was Juan. He gave me an appraising look and said "Good job, Sprite and nice wardrobe." then laughed at his own joke. I wasn't covered by flame anymore. Just like at the hotel, my clothes were gone, did they make holy flame retardant clothes, or at least underwear?

I tried to ignore Juan as I dug in my car for clothes to put on that weren't from the dirty pile. The shirt from Las Vegas and my old jeans would work. I turned back around to Juan, "I thought you weren't supposed to really interfere like the ArchAngels." I said. "I pretty much do nothing but interfere, Balance isn't just a nickname, it is kind of my job Sprite." he said as if I were a little slow. OK so maybe when it came to him I was.

"Why are you calling me Sprite now instead of Cheryl, I thought you said you liked calling things as they were?" I asked actually curious. "I do." was all he said. Not real helpful but I guess it was an answer. Probably more straight forward than if I asked anymore about it. "So what do I do now that the wicked witch is dead? Do I tap my heals three times and find myself in Kansas?" I asked.

"Well, you know that checklist..."

EPILOGUE

I walked slowly into the darker room. The musty smell was everywhere but there was also another more earthy smell that over-powered it. I looked down the cramped aisles until I saw what I came here to do.

The beads hanging from the doorway would fit in a seventies porno. I guess my idea wasn't too far off when my eye's settled on the small naked blonde girl. She was seated in the middle of a ring of candles. She looked so peaceful and beautiful sitting there. She looked like she would sprout more arms in a minute to hold even more peaceful poses.

Sara dropped her fingers just slightly. The moment she did we were plunged into darkness. That was OK with me. I still wasn't used to this whole naked, be free, mentality. The first thing I did when I got out of the shower was put on some underwear of some kind.

Even in the dark I knew she was smiling at me. She was meditating with her eye's closed. They didn't need to adjust to the new light level as much as mine. "I am so happy to see you. Did you take care of everything?" "Yeah, it just cost more than I expected." I replied. I hoped she couldn't see my foot shuffling around or the look on my face. Then I remembered she didn't have to. "Doesn't it always cost us more than we expect?" Sara asked. I still couldn't see her very well but I could hear a light flapping sound as she wrapped herself in something.

She put her hand gently on my arm as she walked by leading back into the bookstore. "I have so much to teach you, but I am afraid I will run out of time before I can finish." "You act like you will die next week." There was some actual worry in my voice. I imagined her confirming the time-line. "No, my life isn't measured in weeks quite yet. Your training will take a long time. I just don't know if I can teach you everything I know. I have no kids so you have to carry what I have learned to the future generations." She said the last part in a strange way. I was getting used to her just knowing things. I also knew she couldn't tell me everything.

"What kind of thing did you have in mind for the first lesson? I'm free for a while. I think." There was something to the set of her hips inside the silk kimono she wrapped around herself. The white and black swirls of the pattern looked antique like most of her books. It was a sharp contrast to her youthful face. "I think first you need to learn how to fall before you learn to balance." That sounded familiar. In all my martial arts classes I was taught how to take a hit and minimize the damage. "OK, what did you have in mind?"

We stood in a wide open park. It was pretty cold but she refused to let me wear a heavy coat. She also insisted I leave the staff in my car. "Try to hit me." she said with a wicked smile. I knew this game. She sure was cocky for a plain mortal. I timed a strike to her ribs. Most people go for the face but that is a vanity and anger thing. I didn't have issues with either of those. I thought I knew what fast was. I was wrong. She caught my arm and in a daze of swirls she left me seated with five fresh bruises.

She leaned down from behind me and planted a kiss on my forehead. "That was fun luv, we will have to try again." I reached up and grabbed both of her shoulders and tossed her in front of me. She didn't get back up right away. Then her body began vibrating. I was sure it was another seizure. I hurried to her side and flipped her over. She lay there laughing in almost hysterical sobs. I could feel a lightness coming from her body. It wasn't perfectly white like an angels, it was more of a bubblegum pink color.

When she stopped laughing she propped herself on one side. "What color did you feel?" I couldn't get used to this mind-reading thing. "Something like a bubblegum pink. Was that an Aura?" "That is pretty close, actually mine is more of a cotton candy pink thank you. At least it is now." I didn't know what to make of the fact that it wasn't always this color. Everything I dealt with had a definite color to it. Demons were black and dark reds, Angels were white and all glowey. "Why can't I just see it like you?" "It has to start with your heart, eventually your mind will catch up. They are different chakras to train. Right now we are focused on your falling though." I am not sure if she started moving while she was still talking or she was so fast I never saw it coming. She swept both legs out and used her bare feet like I would my hands. She swept my feet with one leg and pushed against my thighs with the other. I flew backward and landed in a roll.

We both sat on the ground laughing this time. More bubblegum pink flooding my senses.

Acknowledgments

I would like to thank the following people for teaching me the ropes and pointing out the big crocagators waiting for unsuspecting writers and for the inspiration to follow my dreams.

My wife who has loved me through all the maddening times during development.

My parents and family members for all of their support.

My kids who learned the value of endless tea.

Rebecca Poole, Cover artist extraordinaire at Dreams2Media.

Jennifer Gabbert, Cover model.

Jennifer Randall, Cover photographer.

Chris Killian, Who started my return to writing and a hysterical comedian.

Cory Basil, Author, Artist, Musician and super great guy.

Kory M. Shrum, Author of the Jesse Sullivan series.

S.E. Rise, Author of romance and Horror titles.

Stephanie Bryant Anderson, one of my favorite people and poets.

Heather Donahoe, A wonderful writer and brilliant soul.

Kevin Money, For fighting the tides and being a better human than most.

So many others I couldn't possibly list, but I couldn't live with myself without listing Kyle Gabbert, Naomi Porch ,John Palmer, Tony Bartley, Amy Tucker, Mindy Engle, Shannon Stacey, Jared Schmidt, Amber Martin, Lotus Carroll, Stacy Leiser, Chasity Wingate, David Allen, Patti Yates, Windy Davis-Bentley, Terra Neblett, Christie Killebrew, and the hundreds of others who supported me in one way or another when I needed it.

And to my readers for taking the time to share the start of this adventure, there is much more to come, Thank you!

About the Author

CC Ryburn calls Monterey Bay, California home. He has lived all over the world and isn't finished exploring yet.

He has worked in IT, Bars, Animal processing plants, and everything in between.

He posts semi regularly on ccryburnauthor.wordpress.com and ccryburn.com

If you would like to schedule any signings, conferences, or any other meet and greet, send an email to ccryburn@moralimperativepublishing.com